Slave Ship
and Other Stories

Also by Reggie Chesterfield:
Turned Out!
Black Bra and Panties
Scoundrel

Slave Ship
and Other Stories

By

Reggie Chesterfield

New Tradition Books

Slave Ship and Other Stories
By
Reggie Chesterfield

New Tradition Books
ISBN 1932420657

This book is a work of fiction. Names, characters, places and incidents are either the product of the author's imagination or are used fictitiously. Any resemblance to actual events or locales or persons, living or dead is entirely coincidental.

Florida Sex Party

It was fall and Lesley was getting ready for a party.

The weather, as usual, was hot in South Florida and she was happy that she could wear her favorite sundress without having to bother with bundling up. The convenience of always knowing what to wear had been one of the best aspects of the move for her. Even though she had come from a Southern city, it still got cold as hell there in the winter. Since this was about as far south as she could go in the US without moving to an island, she knew that those cold days were in the past.

Lesley had just recently divorced her husband and had moved almost as soon as the process was final. She had been looking for a change in scenery and the opportunity to put as much distance between herself and her ex as possible. Too many bad memories there. She had caught him looking at porn and that was one thing she could not tolerate. It was just disgusting knowing that he was looking at those dirty movies and websites.

To Lesley, any form of sex that occurred outside of marriage was definitely a no-no and she had had a hard time even looking at her husband after she had found him with that smut. She knew that those people he was looking at couldn't possibly be married because married people don't let people watch them doing something so intimate.

Even though she was still in her twenties, Lesley was considered by some people to be quite old fashioned in her thinking. However, she didn't have a problem with such criticisms. She knew that she was right and would not be dissuaded otherwise.

She had decided not to reconcile with him because she knew that she would never be able to get the idea of him acting like that, like a degenerate getting his rocks off looking at that filth, out of her head. The next thing she knew he would want to start trying that weird stuff out for real in their own sex life. Then he would be like nothing more than an animal trying to climb on top of everything he saw—especially her. This was definitely a road that they weren't going to go down. She had had no choice but to end the marriage.

She still shuddered when she thought about him filling his head with that kind of sordid material. It was though he was some kind of pervert or something.

The party was being held by her boss, Ruby. Since Lesley didn't really know anyone in the area, she saw it as a good opportunity to meet some other people. Also, because she was just getting on her feet, she felt that she couldn't possibly decline the invitation. There was no way she was going to offend her boss. It was the weekend and her first week on the job had gone well so it stood to reason that the party would probably be pretty good too.

After she was ready, she looked at the directions to make sure she knew where she was going and then drove to her boss's house. She had no trouble finding it. It was a big red-brick, Tudor-style, split-level in one of the older subdivisions in the suburbs. The place looked like a combination of every house she had ever watched on TV

Land which was her favorite channel because she could always count on it for wholesome programming. Since the driveway was full of cars, she had to park down the street a little bit, near the intersection where the strip malls started. It looked like a lot of people were going to be at this party. She was glad she had splurged and bought the five liter box of wine to give to her boss at the party. She had to impress because she really wanted to do well at this job. She took a breath, smoothed her dress and rung the doorbell.

"Oh, hello, Lesley," Ruby, said as she opened the door.

Ruby was in her mid to late thirties and was wearing an extremely low cut, short, slinky black dress and fuck-me pumps. It was obvious that she was not wearing any underwear because you could see right down the dress. Her large breasts also served to draw a person's eye to the shortcomings of the garment. She was definitely showing a lot of cleavage and Lesley couldn't overlook the fact that the tops of her nipples were showing. She was holding a glass of wine and was smoking a Virginia Slim.

"We're so glad you could make it. Oooh, you brought wine!" she said in her throaty voice over the sound of the loud music and people talking. She eagerly took the wine from Lesley. Her sexy Florida cracker Southern accent made Lesley feel at home. "This is the good stuff, too!"

"I wasn't sure what you would like so I bought Chillable Red. I heard it's pretty good." Lesley didn't know what to make of how her boss, Ruby, was dressed, but figured that this probably just the way people dressed in Florida, it being so hot and all. Besides, Ruby definitely had the body for it.

"We love this kind. It tastes just like Kool-aid," she said. "Come on in, I'll introduce you to everyone."

Lesley felt good that she was obviously glad that she had decided to come to the party. However, she couldn't help but get the feeling that Ruby was checking her out in a very subtle way. She pushed this thought out of her head. Why would Ruby be doing something like that? Surely it was just her imagination. She was probably just looking at her dress and shoes. Women did that to each other. She knew this from personal experience.

They went into the house which was filled with people laughing, talking, drinking, dancing and having a good time.

As she was walked around the large wood-paneled sunken living room and was introduced to people, some of whom she had seen around at work but had not had a chance to meet, Lesley noticed that almost all the women were dressed similarly to Ruby. Some of them were wearing even less clothing, if that was possible. And they all looked great. While Lesley had a good figure, she almost felt like some sort of frumpy old librarian in her sundress. It was not revealing in any way whatsoever. She was definitely going to have to do some shopping if she was going to fit in down here in Florida.

After making the rounds, they went into the kitchen which was also full of people.

"Hey, Bruce, get over here. I want to introduce you to someone," Ruby said to a shady-looking muscled up, dark-haired guy. He was wearing a tight shirt made out of shiny material and even tighter dress slacks. It was obvious that he was very concerned with his appearance by the way he was dressed, albeit in a very South Florida, oily, overly groomed sort of way.

"Bruce is my husband," she said to Lesley as they made his way over to him.

This made sense from the way he looked, Lesley thought. He and Ruby made a very good-looking, but slightly sleazy couple. He was standing with some other similarly attired men as well as some more skimpily dressed women.

4

He left the group and came over to Ruby and Lesley.

"This is Lesley. You know, I was telling you about her," Ruby said.

"I hope you told him nice things about me," Lesley said meekly and smiled.

"She certainly did," Bruce said, looking her over and smiling. His teeth had been bleached so white that they glowed against the backdrop of his overly tanned skin. "And she was right. You're a very beautiful girl."

He, unlike Ruby, made no attempt to hide the fact that he was checking her out, his eyes lingering on her nicely shaped natural D-cups. It was very clear that he was glad that Ruby had invited her to the party.

"Thanks," Lesley said.

She was a little put off by Bruce because he just kept smiling at her with those phosphorescent choppers. Sure, he was a good looking guy, but the way he looked at her, it was almost like he was leering at her. It made her uncomfortable, but at the same time, she couldn't help but feel just a little bit flattered. She hoped that Ruby didn't get angry at her. She knew how jealous women could get. She looked over at her to make sure. Ruby was fine. She was relieved

"She sure is," Ruby said, putting a hand on Lesley's back and rubbing it while wetting her lips. "She's a great worker, too. She's going to be even better when she gets in the *swing* of things." With that, she and Bruce started laughing.

"What? What?" Lesley asked smiling, not understanding what was going on.

"Oh nothing. You'll find out later," Ruby said. "Here, get something to drink and then let's go back into the living room. I want to introduce you to some more people. I know how hard it must be moving to a new place and all."

"Oh, I'm okay," Lesley said. "I'll just have water."

"You can't just drink water at one of our parties, Lesley. If you don't drink, it makes the rest of us feel like drunks," Ruby said and laughed throatily. She lit another Virginia Slim and pulled a red plastic cup out of a pack that was on the counter and began pouring Lesley some wine from the box. She filled the big cup and handed it to Lesley.

"Okay, I guess. I'm not much of a drinker. I start getting stupid and doing dumb things whenever I drink too much. So watch me, okay?"

"Well, we wouldn't want that," Ruby said. At that, she and Bruce began laughing again.

"What?" Lesley asked again, confused.

"Oh, nothing. Don't worry. Both me and Bruce will be more than happy to keep an eye on you." Then she and Bruce cracked up again.

Lesley stared blankly again. The people standing around them were also snickering. She also couldn't help but notice that they were all staring at her the same way Bruce had. She nervously took a big gulp of wine. Then she took another.

Ruby grabbed the box of red wine. "C'mon, Lesley, let's go mingle," she said and took Lesley's hand and turned to leave. "We'll take the box with us. It'll stay cold forever."

"See you later, Lesley," Bruce said, continuing to leer.

Lesley couldn't be sure but she could almost swear that Bruce was now sporting an enormous erection. She couldn't help but blush. She took another big gulp of wine and tried not to stare. She didn't want to embarrass him by drawing any attention to his boner.

As they walked towards the living room, Lesley was beginning to feel the effects of the alcohol. She couldn't help but comment to Ruby on the way she was dressed.

"I feel like I've dressed for the wrong party with this sundress. If I had known how everyone else was going to be dressed I would have worn something else."

Ruby's eyes lit up. "What you're wearing is fine, but if it would make you feel more comfortable, I would be more than happy to let you borrow something."

"Oh, I couldn't," Lesley said and took another sip of wine. It was really beginning to hit her. She decided then that she didn't mind if she did get a little tipsy. As long as she was able to drive home at the end of the night, she would be okay. After all, she was at a party. Why be a stick in the mud when everyone else was drinking and enjoying themselves? Besides, it would have been rude not to follow her hostess's wishes.

"Sure you can, you're about the same size as me, I think," Ruby said and reached out and started feeling Lesley's body. Her hands lingered on Lesley's breasts, rubbing them gently.

Lesley was almost taken aback, but the feeling wasn't unpleasant. Besides she liked Ruby and didn't want to offend her.

"Yeah, we're just about the same size," Ruby said.

She then took Lesley's hands and put them under hers on Lesley's breasts. She moved them around under her own and Lesley couldn't help but feel a little tingle between her inner thighs. Then Ruby moved their hands over to her own breasts. She took a deep breath and closed her eyes.

"See, we are just about the same up here. There's not much difference at all."

Maybe it was due to the wine, but Lesley didn't jump back in horror. She just went with the flow because she knew that she couldn't do anything else. She didn't want to do anything that could put her job in jeopardy. She rubbed her hands over Ruby's breasts and then put them back to hers.

"Yeah, we're about the same size. We're close anyway."

And Ruby most likely didn't mean anything by it. No point in jumping to conclusions. Besides, how else were they going to tell if they were the same size?

Ruby smiled. "Let's go look in my closet and see what's in there."

Lesley followed, taking another sip.

They walked down a carpeted hallway and then turned into a very large master bedroom which featured a huge mirror that covered an entire wall.

Ruby, still carrying the wine box, walked over to the closet and looked in. "C'mon over here and let's see what looks good."

Lesley obeyed. Now the wine was really making her feel good.

Ruby opened the sliding wood doors and reached in a pulled out an almost infinitesimal silver dress. She held it up to Lesley. "There, I think this will look good on you. It goes good with your jewelry."

Lesley looked at the dress. She had never worn anything so skimpy, but thought that it did look pretty. What the heck, she thought as she held it up to her. It might be fun to wear something like this.

Ruby smiled. "You'll look great. Really sexy. This dress will really show you off." Then she noticed that Lesley's plastic cup was almost empty. "Shit, you're almost out."

Before Lesley could protest, Ruby had filled her cup again. Not wanting to be impolite, Lesley said thank you and took another sip. She wasn't drunk yet, but she was feeling pretty good. She felt like dancing and that was something she never normally wanted to do.

Ruby looked her up and down again. "Now, we need to find you some shoes." She looked at her shoe rack and finally found what she was looking for. It was a pair of what looked like silver stripper shoes. The heels were so high they were almost scary looking. "There these will really show off those legs of yours."

Normally Lesley would never even considering wearing something like this, but in her slightly inebriated state, she was up for it. Besides, they really matched the dress.

"Now, let's get you out of those clothes and get you dressed," Ruby said slyly, putting the wine box on the dresser.

Lesley wondered if Ruby was going to leave to allow her to get dressed, but instead of leaving Ruby walked over and unzipped her dress for her. She walked around Lesley, surveying what she saw and smiling.

Oh well, Lesley thought as she let the sundress fall. Now she was only in her underwear. She reached over and picked up the silver dress and was about to put it on, but Ruby started laughing.

"You can't wear underwear with a dress with like that!"

"But I don't feel comfortable wearing just that dress," Lesley protested. "There's nothing to it. People will be able to see everything."

But before she could say anything else, Ruby had already unsnapped Lesley's bra and had a hand in her panties, pulling them off. Ruby was so fast that Lesley didn't even have a chance to stop her. Now she was completely nude aside from the shoes.

"Now, that's better," Ruby said. "You know, I think you would look good at the party with just the heels. I love the fact you keep your pussy so smooth. I like mine that way too. It just feels so good, doesn't it?" Ruby raised up her dress and showed off her shaved muff. Then she licked her fingers and rubbed it just a little.

Lesley was confused now and didn't know what was going on. She put a hand over her breasts to cover herself up, but Ruby was having none of it.

"Let's stop fucking around and get to it. I'm so horny I can't stand it. If I don't eat that pussy soon, somebody is going to have to lock me up."

"What…?" Lesley said.

But before she could get the sentence out, Ruby had pounced upon her. Ruby had her in an embrace and was kissing her passionately. And she was surprised to feel herself kissing the slightly older woman back. She had never thought about being with a woman before, and maybe it was the wine, but this felt good. And it had been so long since anyone had touched her. In her drunken way of thinking, it was okay to have sex with a woman even if they weren't married, because it wasn't possible for women to be married. So, she went with it. After all, Ruby was her boss.

While Lesley was just taking it all in, Ruby was horny was hell. Her dress now lay in a heap in the floor and she had kicked her heels off. She kissed Lesley's neck and breasts while putting one hand on her pussy. Eventually Lesley couldn't help but respond in kind. She was surprised at the way she was acting, but Ruby was working her over in a way she had never been worked over before. She found herself wanting Ruby's fingers inside of her. She could see that people were walking by the door and looking in occasionally. She was no exhibitionist, but the thought of people watching her do something like this even made her even more turned on. Ruby was just that good. Lesley had only been with her husband in this way, and he had been clueless as to what to do. Ruby however knew her way around a woman. That was for sure.

"Here, lean back on the bed," Ruby said breathlessly and pushed Lesley back. She lifted and spread Lesley's legs and soon had her face buried in her snatch.

Lesley gasped as Ruby went to work. It just felt so good. Did this make her a lesbian? She didn't know but she was so turned on that there was no way she was stopping this until it was over. Just when she was getting ready to orgasm, Ruby stopped. She put two fingers in her pussy and then put them in Lesley's mouth. Lesley eagerly licked them before she even thought about it.

"Let's do me before you come," Ruby said.

Lesley couldn't help but whimper. "But I don't know how. I've never done anything like this," she protested. "Let me come first."

Ruby smiled. "I know you've never done this before. That's why I want you to do me before you come. I want you to want it. I want you to crave pussy. You'll enjoy it better this way, when you're all horny and wanting it."

Ruby had a point, but she had been so close to orgasm. She had loved the taste of Ruby that she had gotten from Ruby's fingers and was really wanting more pussy in her mouth. She was so turned on that she was up for anything at this point.

Ruby rolled over and lay on the bed and guided Lesley's face between her legs. "Just do what comes naturally," she said breathlessly. "There, now, you've got it," she gasped as Lesley began to lick.

Lesley fingered herself as she ate Ruby and could feel herself getting ready to orgasm just from giving cunnilingus. Ruby had been right. She just did what came naturally and did what she liked to have done to her and it must have been the right thing because Ruby was soon holding the back of her head and screaming. Her climax was out of control. This just pushed Lesley over the edge. She found her body convulsing with orgasm.

Ruby crawled down on the bed between her legs. "Now let's give you one that'll make your toes curl."

"But I already had one."

"Well, you're going to have another one. This one will be for real." Ruby grinned wickedly and started licking. Her hands massaged Lesley's big breasts as she sucked.

Lesley was still so turned on that it was just a couple of minutes before she felt her eyes rolling back in her head and her body shaking. This one was even bigger than the last. It was like it was taking over her body. Ruby laughed with pleasure as she got her off.

When the two women were finished and getting dressed, Lesley found that she was feeling a little strange and guilty about what had happened. What had she been thinking? She was no longer drunk and the passion had passed. She almost wanted to run from the room, but she didn't want to offend her boss. She didn't really know what to do. She started to put on her sundress.

"No, Lesley, don't put on that dowdy thing. You'll look like you're going to teach Sunday school. Put on the dress we picked out," Ruby said.

Lesley stared at her. "I'm not a lesbian," she said matter of factly. "I don't think there's anything wrong that you are. But I just wanted to let you know that this is a one-time thing with me. And I think I need to get going."

Ruby cracked up. "I'm not a lesbian either. I'm a swinger. I'm just having some fun. There's nothing wrong with two women getting together and having a good time, is there?"

"A swinger?"

Lesley didn't know what that was. Did it have something to do with dancing and guys in zoot suits? She wasn't sure but she didn't see what it had to do with anything they were talking about.

"I don't know what that is. But you have to understand, I'm not like this. I like men. I'm not interested in doing that kind of stuff with other women. I mean, this was fun and all and I appreciate it, but it's not me. It's not what I do. As I said, this is just a one-time thing for me," Lesley said.

Ruby gave her an "Are you fucking kidding me?" look. Then said, "I think you'll find out pretty soon what a swinger is and as far as a onetime thing goes, we'll see about that." She then gave Lesley a sensuous rub on her perfect ass to accentuate her point.

While slightly offended, Lesley couldn't help but feel herself getting turned on again. What was going on with her? She took a big gulp of wine.

"Oh, I'm just joking," Ruby said. "C'mon, stay at the party. Put on the dress and heels and stay. Remember, we have to work together and I don't want any hard feelings."

Lesley took another gulp of wine. She had to remind herself that she needed this job. She wished now that she hadn't even come to the party. "Okay, but I'm not a lesbian. You'll see that I'm not really like that."

Ruby laughed again and smirked. "Fine, you're not a lesbian."

Lesley got dressed and had to admit that she looked great, albeit extremely slutty. The dress showed everything. Her tits were easily on display and anytime she bent over or took a step everyone could see her shaved pussy. She didn't really care now though she was feeling a little drunk again from the gulps of wine she had consumed. She was determined that she was going to show that she was not a lesbian and if that meant putting herself on display for all the men to look at, then so be it. But still, she couldn't help but feel a little tingle when she saw at how hot she looked in Ruby's dress.

They walked out into the party and it was obvious that the mood had changed. Where people were talking and drinking before, now people were kissing and dancing and many of the women were standing around wearing not a stitch.

Just what kind of party was this anyway? Lesley thought. It certainly wasn't like any of the get-togethers she had been to back home.

Bruce and a couple of other guys walked up. They were equally as well-built as he was and looked almost as sleazy. And as tanned. He put his arm around Ruby and kissed her.

"Hey, we thought we had lost you until we saw you back in the bedroom." He turned to Lesley, "Man, your pussy tastes good." He smiled so wide, his whitened teeth were almost blinding.

"Excuse me," Lesley said, a little bit offended.

"I can taste it on Ruby's lips," he laughed.

Lesley blushed and took another drink. This was certainly not a proper way to speak to a lady.

"That is some of the hottest girl/girl action I have ever seen anywhere, even on pornos," one of the other guys said.

"Why thank you," Ruby said. "Regardless, Lesley has made it clear that she is not a lesbian," she added and rolled her eyes.

"She's not? Well, I don't believe her," Bruce said, still smiling. "I know how you girls are once you get a taste of pussy. You don't want anything else."

"No, I'm not like that. I'm only attracted to men," Lesley said.

"I still don't believe you," he challenged. "I saw what you were doing and I've never seen a girl take to eating pussy like you did. You were insatiable. If you aren't a carpet muncher, I'll eat my hat."

"Well, you're wrong." Lesley said, trying her best to sound confident.

The truth was that she didn't know what to do. What if he was right? She had really loved having sex with Ruby and secretly she was wishing she could do it again. But still, she couldn't get over the idea of just how sleazy the whole business was. She had never felt this way before, so what was different now? Maybe they had drugged her or something? This just wasn't like her. Regardless of her confusion, there was no way that she was going to let Bruce tell her what she was or what she wasn't. She just couldn't stand the way he was so sure of himself about the subject.

"I'll tell you what," Bruce said. "Why don't you show me that you aren't a lesbian? Then I'll believe you. Show me how much you love dick."

Lesley was taken aback. She looked over at Ruby. "Are you going to let him talk to me like that?"

Ruby smiled. "I don't mind a bit. This is something I really want to see. You keep going on about how you're not a lesbian so I want you to show us."

"And I want you demonstrate to us how much you like cock," Bruce said and leered at her. "I won't believe you unless you prove it to me personally."

Lesley looked at Ruby in astonishment.

"Remember, I told you we were swingers. It's what we do," Ruby added.

Lesley's head was spinning. She still didn't understand what Ruby was getting at with this swinger business. How could it be that she didn't mind her husband having sex with her? They were married! She just couldn't comprehend how they could be so nonchalant about sex. Especially with people they weren't even married to!

15

With that Ruby came in close to her and began to nuzzle her neck. Lesley felt her breath quicken and her pussy moisten. She felt her hand going back to Ruby's clit and when she felt Ruby's fingers on her nipple, she knew she was going to have to do something or in a couple of seconds, she would be neck deep in Ruby's pussy. Her decision was now clear.

"C'mon then and let's do it then," she said breathlessly to Bruce

He grinned.

At this moment, she didn't care that she wasn't married to him. She was so turned on she would have fucked a doorknob. The wine she was drinking didn't hurt matters either. Besides, she felt that proving she wasn't a lesbian was more important than keeping her virtue at this instant. He was just so smug, the bastard. She began to walk towards the bedroom, but he stopped her.

"No, we're going to do it out here in the living room," he said.

"But everyone is going to see!" she said.

"That's the point. Everyone at the party saw what you were doing with Ruby and if you want to prove that you like dick, then you'll have to do it in front of everybody."

"Well if that's what it takes, then let's do it in the living room then," Lesley said. For some reason, this now made complete sense to her in her slightly drunken state.

They went into the sunken living room and where there had earlier been a coffee table, there was now a mattress. A crowd stood around it. They were waiting for the show. Lesley became even more turned on at this. She couldn't believe that she was going to do this and had she not been so horny, there was no way she would have. However she was so filled with lust, she simply had to get fucked. She had to have that release. Lesley was aching for sex.

Once they were at the mattress, Bruce turned Lesley around so that she was facing him. "Now prove it to me."

Lesley got down on her knees. Bruce took off his shirt and undid his pants. They fell to the floor and he stepped out of them. Now, his dick was directly in front of her. She was going to prove it to him all right. Regardless, of how much she had liked having sex with Ruby, she was going to make these people see that she liked men, darn it!

All things aside, however, she was still so turned on from Ruby's touch that her body felt like it had electricity going through it. If Ruby's hands had been all it took for her to get going like this, there was no telling she would have done had she had more stimulation. As a result, it was not a problem for her to begin sucking his cock. It was huge though. It was a big, heavy cock and was almost too big to fit in her mouth. It had to be at least nine inches. She fingered herself under her dress as she pleasured him. She got even more turned on fast and did not even mind when the two other sleazy guys who had earlier been hanging out in the kitchen with Bruce undressed and stood around stroking their erect massive cocks.

Ruby sat in a chair nearby and watched with rapt attention. One hand was on her breasts and the other was on her pussy. Most everyone in the room was in a similar position or arousal.

She took turns on the other guys' big cocks. This was just too much, she realized. She was being overwhelmed with lust. The floodgates of her repression had burst. She had to be fucked. She had to feel those big, engorged dicks in her wet twat.

"Give it to me," she said and got on all fours. Bruce smiled.

"Well…how about that?" he said and entered her.

She was so wet; he was able to go all the way in without any effort whatsoever. She was that turned on. He moaned with pleasure when he entered and started pounding her immediately. Meanwhile, the other two guys took turns sticking their dicks in her mouth. She couldn't get enough. Bruce slapped her ass and rammed it in.

Hoots and hollers came from the other people at the party. "Fuck her, Bruce!" and "Make her bark like a dog!" were just some of the things said.

Lesley looked around and saw that the other couples were starting to get it on in due to being so turned on from what she was doing. There were threesomes and blowjobs going on all around the room. She felt her insides tingle and she thrust against Bruce's cock even more. She was tasting the precum from the two other guys now and she couldn't help but start shuddering with orgasm.

"You better keep fucking me!" she said as she came. She held onto the other two guys' dicks to brace herself as she ground it out. She didn't want Bruce to stop before she was finished. Bruce, meanwhile, was starting to sweat.

"I'm going to cum!" he said and began blasting all over her ass.

Lesley rubbed against his dick and balls while he released all his semen.

"Next," she said and one of the other guys started pounding her. She continued to suck the other one, but had to back off a little because she could feel his body starting to tense. She had to have the three of them in her pussy. He could come in her mouth later. She ground against his dick and it wasn't long before she came again. Her big breasts swung as she humped his dick. He didn't last that much longer and she didn't want this cum to go to waste.

"I want it in my mouth," she said and turned around started sucking it.

This gave the other guy opportunity to stick it in. He started out in high gear while the other guy came all over his mouth and face. She couldn't help but swallow most of it. She liked it so much that she had to clean up the rest. Then she could felt the other guy grab her ass and stiffen and she knew that it was time for more cum. She smiled as he blasted his wad all over her face. Since she hadn't been able to orgasm with the last dick, she started fingering herself. She was so hot and bothered that it wasn't enough though and she looked around the room for some available dick. But then she felt a tap on her shoulder. But it wasn't a finger.

It was a strap on. And Ruby was wearing it.

"Do you think you can take this? Or are you still trying to convince me that you're not a lesbian?" Ruby smiled as she stood over her.

Lesley's mouth watered. She was so hot and bothered she couldn't even response. While Bruce and the other guys were huge, this dildo put them both to shame. She raised her head up and licked Ruby's pussy. "I'm not sure if I can take it or not, but I would like to try."

"Then lay down on your back. I want to suck your tits while we fuck," Ruby said.

Lesley lay down and guided the big dildo in. Ruby thrusted against her missionary style and started sucking her tits. Lesley reached up and played with Ruby's massive mammaries while she came closer and closer to orgasm. This one was going to be even bigger than the other ones. She could tell that Ruby was also getting close because of the far away look in her eyes. She was getting off from the pressure from the other end of the dildo against her clit. Ruby fucked her harder than the men had and with the added sensations of her boobs and soft skin, Lesley came again. This time she couldn't help but scream when she came. Ruby began spasming in orgasm immediately following.

After they were finished, Lesley smiled. Then she had a moment of clarity that can only come from too much wine and sex. She was nude, covered with cum and still horny as hell. She felt great and more alive than she had felt in her life. Unlike earlier in the evening, this time she didn't feel one bit of guilt. What the heck had she been thinking then? She hadn't realized just how much she had loved having sex with a woman. How had she been so mistaken about what had been happening to her tonight? Of course, she wasn't a lesbian. It had been just like Ruby had said. They were just two girls having fun together and getting off. She had been too turned on by Bruce's big cock to be a lesbian. She just loved eating pussy too. But *loved* wasn't the word for it. She *craved* it. She couldn't believe what a turn her life had taken tonight. She had started out her usual self, but now she was some kind of lust-filled freak. She now felt bad about divorcing her husband over something as silly as him watching porn—now especially after all she had done tonight. He had called her a prude when he had left and he had been correct. But that was not the case now. She realized that there was nothing wrong with sex and she was going to have as much as she wanted. She had been such a fool but she was over that now.

She looked at Bruce's heavy cock and was wanting it inside of her again and, at the same time, thinking of how much she wanted to eat some pussy when suddenly it clicked. She looked around at all the nude men and women having sex and understood just exactly what kind of party this was. She was also pretty sure what Ruby had been getting at all night.

"Now, I think I know what a swinger is," Lesley said. Everybody around them cracked up and started clapping.

20

All the ladies love Johnny Stiffcock

"I can always tell the dirty girls," Johnny said as he walked into the restroom at the mall.

He was, of course, accompanied by the stacked brunette he had just picked up. Their eyes had met, or rather his eyes had met her breasts and her eyes had met the outline of his semi-hard cock in front of the Chinese place at the food court. He had been harassed by a very pushy Asian lady into trying one of the restaurant's barely edible samples. Fortunately for him, the Asian lady's pushiness was not just limited to him but to the brunette as well.

So when he had got a glance at the girl's copious bosom, the questionable sesame chicken had been well worth the risk of food poisoning. Especially now that they were pawing each other in the family restroom.

"You can? Well..." the young woman said as she moved in a little closer. "Mmmm...your cologne smells nice... Mmmm...smells like Drakkar Noir," she murmured as she began to kiss his neck.

It was actually Polo, but he was just thankful that he had remembered to apply it as his hands moved up and down her body, firmly rubbing her breasts. She wasn't wearing a bra so her nipples were soon protruding out through the fabric of her top. She was the type of woman that should've been encouraged to never wear clothing. She was that well-built. Any vulgarity or obscenity would've more than been overruled by the sheer pleasure seeing her body would give to everybody who saw it.

21

But then again, these same people would have said the same thing about Johnny. At least according to Johnny, this was the case anyway. To him, his big cock and athletic body made him desirable in most people's eyes. Some people, on the other hand, would have said he was scrawny, like he had slight case of worms. However, he thought that he was cut. You could see his muscles after all. Sure he wasn't like a body builder or anything, but he definitely had some definition. So what if you could see his bones? That just meant he was lean, he told himself.

There was one thing, nonetheless, that no one could dispute. Johnny was definitely hung. And that was according to anyone's definition. The fact that he was so skinny just made his enormous penis look even bigger. Straight men weren't even threatened by him, Johnny liked to think. He figured that they looked at his big swinging cock the way they would've looked at their favorite football player whenever he did something great. They were envious, but also in awe.

"Man, I wish I had a big cock like that. I wonder what he can do with it?" they would say.

Woman just looked at it and salivated.

He also liked to fancy that most guys would love to see their girls with a guy like him just to see how crazy the women would get. This is why he never felt bad about having sex with women who were married or in relationships. He figured they looked at him was a like a big cock hero or something. Nevertheless, he always made sure that he never told the taken ones his real name. No need to take any unnecessary chances.

"Mmmm...yes, indeed, I can always tell the dirty ones," he said as her hands found his large, erect cock. "I don't know if it's a look or how you carry yourself, but I can just tell when a girl is game for a little action." He felt under her polyester blend skirt. She wasn't wearing any panties.

"Bingo," he said. "I knew it."

But really it didn't matter to him if girls were dirty or not. Even the best of goody-two-shoes prudes would turn dirty when they saw the imprint of his dick through his Haggar slacks. It didn't matter what their situation—married or single—they all had to have a taste, or at least a feel of his big cock. Good clean, dirty sex. Nothing but fun.

She giggled and lifted up her skirt so he could stick his finger in her already moist pussy.

"Well, you were right this time...mmmm..." she said as he started finger fucking her and stroking his cock. "Are you going to stick that thing in? I've got to be at Hair Castle in ten minutes. Those bitches will give my appointment to someone else if I don't get there on time."

He dropped his slacks.

She turned around and got her first good look at his fully erect member. "Wow, that thing is big!" she said gleefully. "I could tell you were hung through your pants, but man that thing is even bigger than I thought. It's like a third leg or something."

"Well, that's very sweet of you to say so," Johnny said. He was never one to not appreciate a compliment.

She turned back around and presented her pussy. She didn't even have to invite him to start. He stuck it in slowly but she didn't want to take it easy. She started grinding her wet pussy against him and he had no choice but to start giving it to her.

"It feels even better than it looks!" she said as she bucked against him. He didn't really even have to do that much because her lust for his cock was so great that she was doing all the work. She was like a man in reverse as she rammed her pussy on his dick.

23

It wasn't long before she orgasmed, but Johnny still wasn't ready to come so he kept pounding. He knew that she wasn't finished either. So he amped up his efforts. Now it was his turn to fuck. He turned it up and started pounding her. It took her breath away and she moaned from the effort.

"Fuck me!" she said breathlessly.

Her body began to tremble and her big tits were heaving as she had an even bigger orgasm than before. He pulled out and she instinctively knew what to do. She got down on her knees and began to lick and suck his heavy cock. She smiled as he blasted his cum all over her face and in her mouth. He was a heavy cummer so there was a lot of fluid. As a result, she was so coated that she looked as glazed as a cinnamon roll when he was done. At any rate, she had no problem cleaning him up. However, there was still the question of her hair.

"Now I'm going to have get a wash too!" she laughed.

He laughed too. They composed themselves, left the restroom and parted ways.

He almost thought about asking her for her name and number, but then thought better of it. He could always get laid. It happened to him all the time and in the strangest of situations. One time, at a chicken place, this gorgeous black woman had taken a look at imprint of his semi which was showing through his double knits and had been very impressed.

"Your dark snack is free today, baby," she said.

"Why thank you," Johnny said because he knew *it was on*.

"Mmmm...you can't pay my rent if you ain't got that print but I don't think you're going to have a problem with that," she said and licked her lips. "Mmmm...what a big-ass dick! Now that's what I'm talking about!"

Fifteen minute later when she got her first break, they were fucking like a couple of dogs out by the trash bins behind the restaurant. Even though he smelled completely like garbage afterwards, it was one of the better fucks of his life.

Yeah, he never had to worry about getting laid. The ladies always made sure of that. That was because the ladies loved Johnny Stiffcock.

Johnny Stiffcock was what Johnny always referred to himself in his mind. In fact, it was also his email address. He was very pleased with himself for coming up with it.

As Johnny finished his shopping, he thought about the strange allure he had over women. In fact, sometimes it was hard to get things done because it seemed as all eyes were on him. This was because he made no effort to conceal his cock. It was a gift and he thought it would have been a sin not to show it off.

He had never held a regular job other than the one he had had in high school simply because there was no need to. His cock was his meal ticket. Women worshipped and supported him. They would do anything just to get piece of him.

Even so, he also had a side business on the internet where he would go and service lonely housewives out in the suburbs. "Semen Man!" he would say when he rang their doorbells.

He got paid and fucked well on these jobs because these women were so happy when they saw him. They knew they were guaranteed to get a good fucking. He didn't like to think he was a gigolo because in his mind he wasn't. He was just providing a service to women in need. Kind of like a plumber or an encyclopedia salesman, he thought. An encyclopedia salesman who was hung like a horse, that is.

He became more and more turned on as he walked through the mall to the parking garage. He was sporting a semi-erection and as a result could hear the whispers and feel the stares of everyone who saw him. But this was nothing unusual because it happened everywhere he went. This kind of attention only added to the bulge in his pants and the potential for good times with the ladies. The whole thing was like a snake that ate itself, he thought. Just like his penis, except for the eating itself part.

When he got to his Hyundai, he was so horny he couldn't resist the urge to fish it out and start stroking it a little. He was fully erect in seconds. He wasn't too concerned about getting caught because he was just too turned on. A few minutes later, he was thoroughly getting into his jerking off when he heard someone knocking on his window. It was Mall Security.

"Sir, I'm going to have to..." she said in a very husky voice before trailing off.

She was wearing mirrored aviator sunglasses and butch military-style short-cropped blonde hair. Her lean tanned muscular arms flexed with nervous energy and went instantly to her utility belt which was over-laden with a huge walkie-talkie and a big key ring. It was obvious that she was the type of woman who didn't take any guff off anyone, much less a man. She had trailed off because she had gotten a good look at Johnny's fully erect member. Lesbian or not, Johnny's big penis always took the words out of their mouths.

Johnny had been startled when she had tapped on his window but was still too turned on to be as concerned as he should have been. The fact that the security guard happened to be a woman only made him be even more incautious. And hornier. In his state of arousal, she had come right on time.

The obviousness of her sexual leanings had little effect on him.

"Something bit me," Johnny said a little nervously, but still kept smiling. "I was just trying to pull out the stinger."

Nevertheless, he made no attempt to put his penis back into his pants or even to stop stroking it. Besides, this act would have been very difficult considering how large it was fully hard. Putting it back in his fly would have been like sticking a Chrysler into a manila envelope. He knew he was taking a gamble because she could always detain him, but he just had to see how this was going to play out. He had been down this road with many different women before and was intrigued to see that he was having this kind of reaction with this particular kind of woman.

The security guard blushed and her strong hand went to her chest. The open buttons on her knit shirt were a dead giveaway to Johnny. He could tell by the amount of cleavage that she was showing that even though she wasn't into men, she was more than up for a fucking. Regardless of her sexual orientation, she was hot. With a little makeup and different hair and she could have been a fitness model. Even if she was a diesel dyke. As he had stated earlier, he could tell the dirty girls. Oversexed lesbians were no exception.

"You've got to let me suck it," she said gruffly, her eyes glazing over just a little. "I've got have that thing in my mouth."

Johnny smiled and breathed a smile of relief. He had had nothing to worry about all along. The power of his jumbo phallus had obviously trumped her Sapphic inclinations. Even so, he said, "Are you sure about that? I wouldn't have taken you for the kind of girl..."

The security guard grinned and turned off her walkie talkie. "It ain't like I'm dating you. Or fucking you. I'm just sucking you. Besides, if I could get a girl with as big a dick as you, I would just go ahead and call the police on you for jerking off in public like that, you pervert."

"It's good for me that you can't find a girl like that then." Johnny smiled again. It was great how things like this always tended to work out in his favor.

He got out of the car and stepped out of his slacks. He leaned back against the car while the security guard got down on her knees and put her mouth on the head of his cock. It was a good thing that they were in a secluded area of the parking garage because they made no attempt to hide what they were doing. But even if they had been more exposed, it wouldn't have mattered. They would have continued. When a woman is that turned on, she doesn't care who's watching.

And Johnny certainly didn't either.

She moaned as she sucked because she began rubbing herself through her heavily starched Dickies. Johnny was able to see himself in her mirrored shades as she licked his big cock up and down, getting it thoroughly good and wet. She was rough with him, like she was making him pay for the fact that he was a man and she was forced to do that kind of thing to him due to the fact that he was such a freak of nature. She really went to town on it, sucking it so savagely that she took his breath away several times. Johnny knew what was coming next and when the woman deep-throated him, his knees almost buckled. Up and down she went, bringing him closer and closer to orgasm. While this had happened to him before, it wasn't just any woman that could take all of him in her mouth. It was obvious that she had practiced a lot with supersize dildos. He had never realized that having such a butch lesbian suck him off could be so hot.

"Don't pull out when you're about to come. I want the whole load in my mouth," she said breathlessly. She began whimpering a little after that as she brought herself to orgasm with her hand.

By now, her top was unbuttoned enough for Johnny to reach down and rub her nipples. It was definitely one of the best blowjobs he had ever gotten.

"I'm getting ready to shoot," he said.

With that she clamped down on the head of his dick to form and airtight seal. He grabbed the back of her head, and soon he was squirting. Even though he had already orgasmed earlier that day, he still had quite a load left and the woman eagerly swallowed every drop.

When they were finished, Johnny pulled up his pants and the security guard buttoned up her top.

"If you want to fuck sometime," Johnny said. "Feel free to find me."

She laughed and ran her hands through her crew cut. "So fucking typical," she said as she shook her head.

Then she leaned in and grabbed him by the balls. "You tell anyone about this, I'll find you and choke you with that big dick of yours." She twisted them a little and smiled. "I can't let that kind of thing get out about me, you know? I don't want people to get the wrong idea."

Johnny laughed nervously. "Sure, I won't say anything. I promise."

"Good," she said and let go of his balls. "I just had to make sure that you understand that this is just a onetime thing. I just had to give it a try, you understand?"

With that she punched him on the shoulder and walked off.

Johnny breathed a sigh of relief and got in his car. He smirked to himself because knew that this wasn't the last he would see of the security guard. She was just too into it. As far as keeping his mouth shut, he planned on posting the full account of it on his webpage. He couldn't keep his good fortune at finding a lesbian who was in the closet in regards to her love of dick to himself. So what if she found out about it? She would be angry at first, but she would get over it because he knew that he had what she wanted, what she hadn't even known that she had to have.

He was so thankful that the ladies did indeed love Johnny Stiffcock.

Common workmen

Caroline was mortified as she walked back to work from the deli. She had just had a bowl of soup which the waitress had just happened to spill on her purse when she had served it.

And not just that, the waitress had also stepped on her foot in the process of cleaning up her mess thus scuffing her brand new tan Naturalizers. As a result, she was in no mood for this crap. She had just wanted to hurry back to the office and get back to work. She wanted to bury herself in the mundane details of her so-called career of managing a marketing department. But now this? On top of everything else, she was now being sexually harassed. It made her want to duck her head and hide.

Here's what happened: After she had left the deli, she had walked by a construction site and had been singled out by the men working there. It was a building that was being renovated by a small crew of workers. Sweaty, dirty construction workers who probably stunk to high heaven of nicotine and stale beer. And body odor. These were guys that probably lived in trailers and drove pick-ups. These were guys who looked at porn and blew their paychecks on lottery tickets and buffalo wings. These were guys who got their food from those ptomaine wagons. There were just filthy common workmen.

How dare they speak to her like that? She was a career woman after all. An executive. She had a degree and made more money than them. If she had been their boss, she would have fired them all.

Even though they had good bodies and looked good with their shirts off, there was no excuse for what they had said to her. How they had acted towards her.

She referred to them in her mind as *common workmen* because that's the way she had been taught by her upper middle class parents. She had been brought up to view such characters as such, as *common workmen*. Men who worked with their hands rather than their minds. Men who you hired if you had to have something done around the house like cleaning the gutter or fixing the toilet. Men who couldn't or wouldn't do any other sort of work because they were either too stupid or too lazy.

They were definitely not the type of men she would ever date. If she was even still into that kind of thing, that is. She had freed herself of the problem of dating when she had convinced herself that she was an independent single woman who had no need of anyone, much less a man. Even to date. Or fix a toilet for that matter. She could take of that herself just fine, thank you.

When she had walked by, the workers had run to a window and started hollering and whistling at her like she was a piece of meat rather than the strong independent professional she considered herself. They acted like she was on display for them. It was like they all wanted to jump on her and start fucking her like she was a bitch in heat and they were a bunch of dogs. What was most ridiculous to her was the fact that she was wearing her most conservative,

31

unflattering business suit. How could they find that sexy? Didn't they get it? Couldn't they tell that she was above that kind of thing? She just couldn't see how it was possible that they had been able to tell what a great body she had even through that unsexy outfit. They probably acted like that around all women. Those men were no better than animals.

"Hey, baby, do you want to hang on my flagpole?" one of them hollered and grabbed his crotch.

"Bend over and touch your toes, mama!" a Puerto Rican looking guy yelled and acted like he was slapping her ass. "I want to see you put your palms on the floor!"

That and other ridiculous stuff like that was yelled at her. Were they even serious about this stuff? What woman would find this kind of stuff appealing in any way, shape form or fashion? Regardless, she couldn't help but blush bright red. It was just so embarrassing. Those men hooted and catcalled at her like she was there for their enjoyment. Catcalling. What a ridiculous term, she thought. She had never called her cat like that.

"Common workmen," she snorted to herself bitterly. "Not good for anything."

Normally, she would have been walking with some of her fellow managers, but this time she had been alone because she had had to work through her usual lunchtime. She continued to walk, going as fast as she could without running so that she could get out of their line of vision. She was so embarrassed that she swore she would never go to that deli again, even if it was her favorite place to eat. There was no telling what she might say to them the next time. She would really give them a piece of her mind and they wouldn't be too happy about that. That was for sure.

"Hey, baby, why don't you back that ass up?" another of them cackled. "I need to do a booty inspection."

"Mmmm...baby, what I would do to get my mouth on them big titties!" This big black guy licked his lips in a very exaggerated way to show what he was going to do to her breasts.

She couldn't help but shudder with disgust.

Eventually Caroline turned the corner and was out of their sight. Even so, she continued to boil over as she rushed back to her building. After she got there, she buried herself in some reports and stewed about what had happened to her.

She had always been a little self-conscious of her body. Not because she was ashamed of it or anything, but it always seemed to draw more attention to her than she wanted. She was blessed with large breasts and had kept herself in shape. She hadn't let herself go the way a lot of women her age had. She was just a little embarrassed by the way the men had acted towards her.

However she hadn't ever let these feelings keep her from working out. But to what purpose? she often asked herself as she forced herself onto the treadmill. She certainly wasn't trying to impress a man or anything. It was just part of her routine which she followed religiously. Eventually though, the toils of her job began to consume her and the events of the day were pushed from her mind.

That night as Caroline walked into her apartment and threw her purse on the couch, she sighed heavily. She went to the refrigerator and fighting the urge to open a pint of Ben and Jerry's, poured herself a glass of wine. Better drunk than fat, she thought.

As she went through her mail, she couldn't help but also look back at her life. This was something she had been doing a lot lately and always with extreme disappointment. It was always when she returned home to her empty apartment that doubts about what she had done with her life would begin to sink in. When her façade of being a single, independent career woman would begin to crumble and the darkness of her reality would make itself known.

Simply put, she was alone and sometimes she couldn't help but become depressed about it. At times like this, it was hard to find a silver lining. She had held such promise as a young woman that it was almost unfathomable that she had ended up in such a state.

As she looked over at the well-worn dating books that were stacked up on her coffee table, it was even more evident that she was rapidly approaching forty and by all appearances had done little with her life. She lived in a crappy little apartment in the city that smelled so strongly of cat that it would have overwhelmed most people. Sadly, she didn't even notice it anymore. Some of her small town acquaintances thought that her having an apartment in the city was really neat, but this was no consolation. They thought of her as being this successful single woman who was independent and didn't need anyone. But this wasn't comforting either.

Sure, she had the freedom of being alone, but most of the time it just wasn't what it was cracked up to be. She, of course, had a cat, a gay neighbor whom she hated, but not because he was gay but because he was an asshole, a Japanese car, a 401k plan and a career that had stalled at mid-management. She had hit the glass ceiling about ten years earlier and there was no way that she was ever going anywhere now. What had happened to the dreams she had held in college? She was going to go into the entertainment industry. She was going to work in the movies. She was going to travel the world. But, alas, nothing like that had happened. She had foolishly put all her youth into her career and her career, if one could call it that, was now all she had. No family, no friends other than those at work and no prospects.

Caroline had always thought that she would be married someday, but had never had the time to commit to a relationship. She had always looked for Prince Charming, but had never even remotely found anyone that could measure up. As a result, she had simply gone on dates. Lots and lots of dates. As good looking as she was, she had never had a problem getting asked out by successful eligible men. Sometimes there was a small spark and she had gone out with the same one for several years. She had even lived with a lawyer named Jeffrey for a little over a year right after she had moved to the city. Things had gone well until he had one morning suggested that she get up and cook him breakfast. She had taken this slight to her career-woman status personally and had kicked him out immediately. She wasn't going to be anybody's maid.

But that was much farther than her relationships had usually gone. Normally she went no further than dating these men. Sure, she sometimes had sex with them. At least some of them. Generic, vanilla sex. But it hadn't really been something she had really enjoyed. Sure it was fun while she was doing it, but afterwards she had always felt used. Like she had been coerced or something. Like it had been something that one was supposed to do in a relationship. Or after one had dated a person for several times. She hadn't even been a success at screwing and that was something that should have been easy. Truth be told, that was the real reason why she had formulated the independent woman persona and had said goodbye to dating.

Such thoughts made her even more miserable. She drank more wine and went to bed.

The next day was Saturday and she didn't have to work. The light of day pushed away the gloom she was feeling the night before and she awoke in a different frame of mind. Her cat, mercifully, had let her sleep in. This was a rare occasion because Fluffy usually pounced on her head at dawn each morning. While she loved the fact that Fluffy liked her enough that she awakened her to play, sometimes she wished she could just boot that damned animal out the window. Sometimes she saw the cat as a symbol of her frustrated life, but this was only in her darker moments. She didn't feel like this now. She loved the cat at this particular moment. Fluffy had let her get some rest, after all.

As she took a shower, Caroline couldn't help but think about how those men had acted at the construction site. She couldn't get the sight and sounds of those low class lunks hooting and hollering out of her mind. She thought about them with their sweaty bodies and tight t-shirts grabbing their crotches and wagging their tongues at her. Those uneducated common workmen.

It was weird, but while it had offended her then, she, for some reason, found it strangely exciting now. Maybe it was because her hormones were up because she had had a good rest, but thinking back, she couldn't help but feel a little flattered and a lot turned on by how they had acted like a bunch of animals when she had walked by.

As she continued to shower she couldn't help but become excited at the thought of the men. She blushed and was embarrassed, but at the same time she quickly found herself getting wet. And not just from the water. As she began to rub her clitoris, she found her thoughts progressively getting more and more heated. Her mind went down strange paths as she thought about the incident. Stuff she had never thought before began racing through her mind. Before this, her fantasies had mainly fallen along the lines of romance novels where she was taken captive by swarthy buccaneers, fallen noblemen and desperate outlaws. But not this time. This time it was more real. More sexual. More carnal. This time her thoughts ran to situations that could really happen. Rather than one-on-one sex, she was lusting to have all men on her at once. Each one taking his turn at her. Every single, filthy, dirty-minded common workman at the site. In her mind, she would have one man's dick in her mouth as another one fucked her from behind. Meanwhile, she would be giving a handjob to another. Her breath quickened as she thought about the men's rough hands all over her breasts. She rubbed her nipples hard as she thought how they would manhandle her. How they would treat her like something they were working on rather than a person. They would use her like one of their tools they used to build things. But instead of construction, she would use her to achieve their pleasure. Her inner thighs quivered at how she would work their cocks. Her breath quickened as she moved her hands over her breasts and ass, finally settling on her pussy. She thought about how they would eat her twat the way they ate their sack lunches. Her wet body was slick from soap and it didn't take long for her to come.

After got out of the shower, she was a little ashamed at what she had fantasized about.

I'm not like that, she thought. She wasn't even a sexual person she reminded herself.

Nevertheless, while she ran her errands that day, she couldn't help but think about her fantasies. It was almost all she could do not to rub herself in public. Especially when she had taken her cat to the veterinarian for yearly vaccinations. While her kitty was getting worked on, she ached to work on her own kitty. The thought of being fucked by multiple common workmen made her so hot that she could feel herself oozing through her granny panties and loose, shapeless denim shorts. She had gotten so worked up in her lustful thoughts that she had had to go to the restroom and pleasure herself. If the veterinarian hadn't been about eighty-years old, she would have jumped on him instead, but she wasn't quite ready to go there—yet.

After Caroline completed all she had to do that day, she went home. As she walked aimlessly around her apartment thumbing through fashion magazines, it occurred to her to do something she had never done before. It was probably because she was still horny as hell, but this time she didn't feel ashamed at all for her feelings. She got on the internet and started searching for porn. Most especially *gangbang* porn. She had never done this sort of thing before and found herself almost salivating as she searched the internet and found what she was looking for. Her hand was on her pussy even before she could look at any pictures. And when she opened a new window dealing with home improvement topics she almost convulsed with pleasure. She orgasmed many times that evening and knew that this was indeed something she could get into.

And this was how her life went for the next few weeks. She would work all day and rush home and look at porn and masturbate. She actually began to get excited about going home. She had used to tell herself that she couldn't wait to get home to see her cat, but deep down she knew that wasn't true. It was just an excuse. Something to fool herself into thinking that she wanted to go home. However, now she had something that really made her feel good. Sure she was still a little bitter about how her life had turned out, but now at least she had something to look forward to. Hadn't she always heard that having something to look forward to was a cornerstone to being happy? Well, at least she had that now. She loved to see pictures and videos of women taking on all sorts of men. Men these women didn't even know. She also found herself even getting into women having sex with other women, but the gangbang was what really turned her on. She even joined some groups online to find out more.

She was definitely hooked and felt happier than she had in a long time. People at work even noticed her new attitude. She even bought some sex toys online. While her favorite was the rabbit, she especially loved the small bullet-type vibrator that she could wear under her clothes. This way whenever the urge hit, she could discreetly turn it on and *scratch her itch* so to speak.

It wasn't long before her new habit began to creep into her dressing habits. She began to shop for more revealing and form-fitting clothes. While before she looked like she was wearing maternity wear because her clothes were so baggy, she now wanted to show off her tits and ass. This was a major step, but she was so turned on by the porn and her fantasies that her sexuality couldn't help but come out of her in different ways. She was especially fond of a short skirt and tight sweater combo. The lower cut the better. Her goal now was to make men drool which had been next to impossible when windsuits had been her preferred casual-wear.

She even bought new work clothes. While she had tried to hide her breasts before, now she made sure she showed off her cleavage at almost every opportunity. She bought clothes that showed off her body as much as possible without crossing the line into unprofessionalism. She still had to make a living. And she had to maintain her image as an independent career woman. This was a very important aspect of her identity after all.

Still she managed to achieve her purpose. Every look she got from a man would start her heating up. She made a point of going by the construction site to see what they would do. If they had hooted at her before when she wore what she now regarded as the unsexiest clothes imaginable, they were literally beside themselves now. The men almost lost it this time. They hollered and jumped around like a bunch of gorillas trying to grab a banana off a hook in the ceiling. She could almost hear the whine in their voices. The whine that comes with someone who is so horny that he is doing his best to keep his hands off his cock.

"Hey baby, I've got a corporate ladder for you to climb!" one of them yelled as he pretended to beat off.

Mmmm...Caroline thought. I bet he does. *The filthy common workman.*

Even though they were quite a ways away, she was sure that she could see their dicks growing in their dirty work pants. She could just imagine how her fantasy would come true if she just went over there. She fought the urge because, while she was as horny as hell, she wasn't sure how something like that would play out in real life. For now, she would just have to be content with her vibrator.

After one particularly rewarding session of watching porn, she suddenly realized something.

Why couldn't she get involved in the action?

Maybe not to do actual porno, but maybe leave her apartment and see what happened? Just get out and go with the flow and let the situation come to its logical conclusion. She wanted to see if her fantasies could become reality if she just let nature take its course. Surely it couldn't be difficult. She saw her porn addiction as the best thing that had happened in her life since she had gotten a coffee mug for two years consecutive good attendance. Why not go further with it? She would have to be careful where she went. But she would just have to trust her instincts.

It was decided. She had had regular one-on-one sex before, so why not go for it and seek out some group action? She could think of no reason why not.

She grabbed her vibrator and fired up the internet again to explore the logistics of setting up a real life encounter.

But then she realized something and turned it off.

She didn't need an internet to find what she was looking for. She would go to the construction site. She would give those common workmen something they could work on. They could definitely work with their hands on her. She looked forward to slumming it.

She squirmed as she began to get heated up. This was probably the first time she had had a good reason for wanting to go to work the next day.

The following day, she wore her sexiest work outfit and couldn't help but absent-mindedly go about her job. She left her underwear at home because she didn't want anything getting between her and all those cocks. She hadn't really been sure what to wear, but figured if real life was anything like her fantasies, she wouldn't be wearing them for long once she approached the workers.

She fidgeted all morning because couldn't wait to go to lunch.

"Caroline, is there anything wrong?" her boss, the department director, had asked after he had stood in front of her desk for a couple of minutes without being noticed.

He was a soft, shapeless doughy man characterized by his cheap shoes and pleated khakis. He was definitely not a common workman by any stretch of the imagination. She now realized why her sex life had always been so terrible up to this point. She had always dated guys like him.

"Oh, nothing. I've just got something on my mind," she answered truthfully, flustered that he had taken her mind off her fantasies.

"It must be something pretty important. As deeply in thought as you are," he said.

"Oh, it is," she said and smiled. Fortunately for her, he had to run off to a meeting.

She fingered herself under her desk until she knew that it would be safe to leave. She quickly left her building and walked over towards the site and stopped just as she approached the building. She was very nervous about going into it and almost turned around and went back to her office several times but her horniness won out. She had a secret fear that the men might think she was a fool, but then realized that such thinking was stupid. What man would turn down an opportunity like this? Especially men who acted like them. These were men who were accustomed to things like bologna sandwiches with mayonnaise. A woman like her would be like a filet mignon to them.

She walked into the site and heard voices but didn't see anyone. She followed them up the stairs until she found what she was looking for. It was a large empty room. She noticed that there were three men there. Where had the others gone? All the ones who had hooted and hollered at her? It didn't matter. Three would be enough.

They didn't notice her at first but when she walked up to them, they couldn't help but whistle under their breath. They were all sweeping up and picking up debris in a way that suggested that they had probably been sweeping and picking up the same debris for hours in an effort to ride the clock. The place looked almost finished but was still quite dusty. She noticed immediately that they were focusing upon her like she was a piece of meat. She could feel her pussy tingling with excitement. Her breasts were aching to be groped by hands other than her own. By their common workmen's hands. Yes, this was going to be a good day, she could feel it.

"Can I help you?" a short, muscular Puerto Rican said to her in heavily accented English. He wasn't really that short, but he was shorter than the others. Even though he was built like a beer keg, he didn't have an ounce of fat on him.

"Actually I think you can," Caroline said. She looked him in the eye and casually pulled up her skirt, revealing her shaved pussy. "I was wondering if you guys might be able to help me with a problem I've got. It's the kind of job that only common workmen like you can do. But first of all I need to know if you have some tools about this big?" She held her fingers about ten inches apart. "You'll need them for the job I need you to do."

The Puerto Rican grinned and looked over at the other guys who almost ran over to join him. One of them was a muscular young trashy tattooed white guy with a ponytail who, in Caroline's opinion, looked like he should have been in jail and a tall black guy who looked like he had just awakened from a nap.

What a lucky girl I am, Caroline thought. She could tell that these guys were going to be able to give her what she needed. They were so eager and horny. They were like dogs, she thought. She couldn't help but start juicing at this thought.

"I don't know if we're common workmen, but I think we can help you. And we've definitely the tools you need," the Puerto Rican and grinned again.

The term *common workmen* had sailed over their heads, she chuckled to herself. However, her reference to their *tools* hadn't. What filthy uneducated minds they had, she thought. She looked at their dirty clothing and fingernails and couldn't wait to get her hands dirty.

"I know that's right," the black guy said and grinned.

He was already getting hard. She could tell that he was hung like a horse. He was just like one of the guys she had seen in the porno clips she had been watching.

"Where's all the other guys that were here before? Every time I walk by here you all start yelling and hollering at me. I was hoping that all of you would be here."

43

"That was you? I thought I recognized you," the white guy said, lighting up a cheap cigarette and scratching his head.

"Everybody else has moved on to the next site. We're just cleaning up," the Puerto Rican said, lying. It was obvious that they were just goofing around. "But I think there's enough of us to handle this job.

"I'm sure there is," she said and grinned and figured that it was now or never.

She looked at the guys again. She had never really fantasized about a black man or a Puerto Rican, but these three guys made her so horny she wanted to strip off and start masturbating on the spot. Her first group experience was going include some interracial as well as multi-cultural action. Pluralism? Wasn't that the term she had heard in her government class? It probably didn't mean anything like this though. The thought of the screwing she was going to get almost took her breath away.

The guys smiled at each other. They started laughing and she started laughing too. She wasn't really sure how to get things started, but just decided to do what nature dictated. She wanted to get next to them. She wanted their cocks. She moved in close to them and the black guy reached out and rubbed her ass. She didn't resist. She said something about them looking good and the white guy moved in close and put his hand up her short skirt and began to rub her pussy. He was pleased that it was already wet.

"I'm glad you ain't wearing no panties," he said.

"I knew I wouldn't need them," she laughed.

She reached out and felt the Puerto Rican's crotch and was happy to feel that he was already semi erect. And he had a big one. It was probably about seven inches, but it was wide. Almost like a beer can. It suited his muscular body.

44

They all moved in closer to her and began to nuzzle her neck and rub their hands up and down her body. The black guy and the white guy were behind her and the Puerto Rican was in front. Her hands were on their cocks and she loved the fact that they were already hard. She just kept getting wetter and wetter. She almost couldn't stand it. She was so worked up now, she was going to have to have some dick.

"I think you look like you could handle the three of us pretty easy, baby," the black guy said as he rubbed her pussy, sticking two fingers in.

She laughed. She didn't know for a fact, but she was pretty sure that she could go through the three of them like a hot knife through butter.

She was ready now. She was ready to fuck and have her fantasy fulfilled right there in the empty building. She had her clothes off in what seemed like seconds. She lustily pulled the Puerto Rican's cock out of his workpants. It was completely hard now and she started sucking it like she had never seen a cock before. It was so wide that she had a hard time getting her mouth around it, but she managed somehow. Her sexuality was coming in full bore and she was aching to be fucked. She just had to have all these guys inside of her. Her wish was soon granted because the white guy soon was fucking her doggie style while they stood right there in the middle of the room. His dick was big too.

"Give it to me you fucking common workman! Fuck me like you're trying to get out of paying child support!" she yelled.

The trashy white guy really picked up the pace.

She felt so lucky because she was having sex with such well-hung men at the same time. The black guy stroked his dick and rubbed her breasts while the others fucked her. She knew that he was going to be last. He was going to really put her though her paces. He was by far the biggest of all of them. His dick was so large that it didn't even stand up when it was fully erect. It hung down like a rolled up sock and the thought of fucking him made her fuck and suck even harder. She came rapidly from the fucking what the white guy was giving and when she began to taste precum from the Puerto Rican's beer can cock, she knew it was time for them to switch.

She looked around and saw a tarp lying on the floor. This was as good as anything to lie on and took the opportunity to get on her back. She now wanted it missionary style. When he put that cock inside of her, she gasped because she had never had such a filled up sensation. The taller black man then presented her cock to her to suck while the white guy rubbed her breasts. She hungrily sucked that enormous cock and she couldn't wait to get it inside of her. She ground against the wide cock and came shortly thereafter.

The black guy grinned as he switched places. She watched with anticipation as he pushed it inside of her. She wasn't even sure if she could take it all or not, but she did and he started fucking her like she was another guy's girlfriend. She came instantly and then she came again as he pumped her. She sucked both the white guy's cock and the thick beer can cock while he worked. Finally, he was ready and she was exhausted. She was still horny as hell and wanted their jizz in her mouth.

"I want to suck you all off," she said, possessed with lust

The three men were more than happy to oblige. She sucked them each off, letting each one cum in her mouth, face and tits. This turned her on even more and she had to masturbate to another orgasm after they were finished.

She lay there for a second, looking at the well hung men standing over her, with their dicks hanging. She couldn't help but start laughing. "I did it! I actually went through with it!"

"Damn!" said the black guy. "You sure did. I ain't never seen a girl as horny as you. Shit!"

"You probably won't either," she laughed.

"Anytime you want to go again, just give me a call," the white guy said. "I'll let you know where you can pick me up."

"You don't have to worry about that," she said. "But next time, you need to bring a few more men."

"Mmmm, that won't be a problem, baby," said the Puerto Rican. "I'd love to stick it to you anytime."

She giggled. She was so pleased with herself, she couldn't stand it.

As the days passed after the event, she had thought that she might feel a little guilty about what she had done, but instead, felt really good about it and couldn't wait to do it again. Her upper middle-class parents would be so appalled that she had allowed herself to be associated, much less gangfucked by such a group of uneducated, ambitiousless men. Guys her family looked down their noses at. She tingled with the thought. She had truly enjoyed getting a big of rough.

Then one day while she was at the office daydreaming about being gangbanged by a group of well-hung dry wall hangers, it dawned on her.

She had done it.

She had turned her life around without even realizing it. Her life was no longer going nowhere. She was no longer drab, but filled with color and life. And she no longer thought of herself as a failure. She had found her niche. Besides, compared to those common workmen, she was definitely a success. In fact, she was what they thought of as a high class woman. And that made her feel even better about herself. So what if she was condescending to them? It made her feel good and that was what was important. Besides, they more than got their fair share in the deal. Just because she felt superior to them didn't mean she couldn't use them to have a little fun.

She now realized that happiness follows when you find yourself doing something that you're truly good at and enjoy. A person is happy because they've found what they're supposed to be doing. Her problem had been that it had taken her a long time to find it.

Caroline may not been a success in other facets of her personal life, but she could be a successful slut. And if this was what worked for her and she enjoyed it, she was going to be as slutty as possible. The world was her oyster and she was happy to let go of her old baggage. To get rid of all her old notions of what she should be doing with her life.

Her life was now exciting and happy. Misery no longer consumed her. And all due to some filthy common workmen. She chuckled to herself. She might even start dating again. Why not? But this time she wouldn't be so picky. In fact, she would only go after the meatheaded, common workmen types. Men who were good with their hands. And cocks. After all, in addition to the sex, she did have some things to fix around her apartment.

And now she could get rid of that damned cat.

Well-jugged

Jugsy couldn't help but create a scene wherever she went. Her body dominated every situation and her curves compelled people to look. Dicks would rise to the occasion and women who were so inclined—and even some that weren't—would have to fight the urge to start rubbing themselves. She was their one exception when it came to girl/girl sex. Anyone who didn't feel this way was just jealous, at least this is what she told herself. After all, who couldn't appreciate someone like her on a sexual level? Every jerkass from hell west to Crockett who saw her had to check himself to keep from copping a feel of her luscious body. It was just so tempting to try to get next to her, to rub against her, to grind against her. She was pure sex on legs. Her ass was smoking, but her tits…man, her tits were indeed something else.

In other words, she was what you would call, *well-jugged.*

Yes, Jugsy's breasts were large and so well shaped that it was shame to put them in clothes. Not just a little big, but so big and so nice that nothing she wore could really cover them up. They were the type of breasts that would make even the most stale and limp-dicked of the old, infirm and disinterested salivate whenever he saw them. They were so big that one boob was as big as a grown man's head. A grown man with a large head, no less. A miracle of nature? A miracle of science? Who knew and who cared? Those things were huge.

And she was definitely not ashamed of her assets either. She loved showing those melons off. Besides there was nothing she could wear that could conceal them even if she wanted to. As a result, she made no effort whatsoever to keep them under wraps. Anything she wore somehow seemed just a little obscene. Just a little dirty. She would have swelled up a muumuu.

She just couldn't dress in any way that wasn't suggestive. Nor did she want to. As a matter of course she always made sure to show off at least a little cleavage. However she especially loved wearing cut off t-shirts which showed off her *undertit* as she referred to it. Regardless of what she wore, she couldn't help but be on the fine line of being just barely obscene. Just dirty enough to get people to look but not dirty enough for them to call the cops.

But what really got her off was giving people an eyeful. To let them get a good look at what she had to offer. "Oops, excuse me," she would say as she squeezed past people when she would get in an elevator. "Ooh, pardon me," she would purr when she stepped past other shoppers in the shampoo aisle at the K-Mart.

She always made the effort to go into the male dominated areas of the department stores whenever she went shopping because she never wanted to miss an opportunity to show off. She would make any excuse to go to the auto parts or home improvement sections. She lived to show off her heavy hangers. And when she went to the camping section, it was always certain that there would be plenty of tents pitched.

Needless to say, she always made a point to wear tight clothing to show off her assets to their utmost effect. If her breasts didn't make those dicks stiffen up, her ass and legs would. Her objective was to make men get obvious hard-on's and she was usually successful. Whenever she noticed that a gentleman was sporting a boner, she would make sure that she would linger so that he got a really good look. Oh how the polyester would strain while she would bend over even more so that he really get a gander at her big babies.

The thought that men would be stroking their meat to her made her even wetter. Her panties would be drenched by the time she would be finished shopping. She could just imagine how much these men wanted to put their hands on her tits. How much they wanted to rub them, how much they wanted to put their big dicks in between them and shoot their loads all over her massive mammaries. The notion of what they wanted to do with the rest of her body would just put her over the top. She fantasized that these men were sitting in lonely, dingy badly decorated hovels thinking about her while they jacked off. This made even more turned on. She was happy to be at least one bright spot in what she saw as their otherwise miserable lives.

She was just too much package for one person. She reveled in her sexuality and the effect she had on people. She loved the fact that most people had to masturbate when they saw her. She too had to masturbate when she thought about it. To think about them fantasizing about her sucking cock and getting fucked made her fantasize about sucking cock and getting fucked. And eating pussy and getting jism blasted onto her big jugs. It was just too much to keep her hands off herself most of the time. It was just a dirty sexual loop that she was caught in.

This was fine though because masturbating was one of her favorite pastimes. She loved to fondle her breasts while she rubbed herself and sometimes she was just so turned on that she would overheat her vibrator. When this happened, she would have to sit on the dryer just to finish. Or put her cell phone on vibrate and call herself over and over again—while the phone was in her panties. Anything to knock the edge off so she could finish whatever business she was up to.

While showing off was enough to get her juicing, the thought of actually banging some of these guys had occurred to her on several occasions. She was quite picky but a few years earlier had gotten it on with an extremely well-hung blonde headed guy at the garage when she had been getting her car (and ultimately herself) serviced.

But he had been the exception. And that was only because he had been so muscular and so well-endowed that she had allowed herself that indulgence. She also figured that he wouldn't be smart enough to find her if she wanted to ditch him after the screwing.

While the guy was a little greasy and somewhat simian in appearance and behavior, he had been good. He was a real knuckle-dragger, but she didn't care. She wasn't screwing his brain after all. He had bent her over in the men's room and had really drilled her. She was very turned on otherwise she would have been appalled by the horrid conditions of the facility. She couldn't keep from screaming then, as he plowed into her, while holding onto her tits. Luckily, she had worn a short skirt and tank-top that day so he had easy access to both erogenous zones. He had pounded her and sucked her nipples so well that she had orgasmed twice before he had even started on her doggy style.

"You, dirty grease monkey!" she had gasped when he started nailing her. Her boobs were so big that when they swung, she almost lost her balance. But her pussy had too good a grip on his cock to let that happen. She let him ride her like a rented scooter and when he kicked it up a notch and really started going deep, she couldn't help but squeal.

He reached around and grabbed her tits and thrusted even harder. At this he began to grunt and make noises that seemed to come from one of the more primitive part of his make up.

When that happened, she couldn't take it any more and that's when she started howling. She also loved the fact that he had asked before he came on her tits. A perfect gentleman, she thought and had allowed him to do it. He came a lot too, and she was more than happy to use her mouth to clean him up. She just left his cum on her tits because she knew that she would stay turned on even after she left and would want to use her vibrator afterwards.

But this was the exception. Just showing off her body was usually enough.

No, Jugsy didn't regularly pick up random men. She was too much of a lady for that. The thought of what they would want to do to her was enough. She liked being able to just show off her jugs. Her vibrator and dildos were good enough and whenever she needed a little something extra to release the pressure, she could always locate some meathead to work on her car.

Yes, Jugsy was built for sex. Plain and simple. It's just what she was made to do. The fact that dirty old men stared bug-eyed at her wearing tube-tops and tight sweaters didn't bother her. It turned her on to be such an object of lust. Being well-jugged came with responsibilities and she was more than happy to honor them.

She only wished she could find a brassiere that fit.

Some might call it a sickness...

"It looks like the place is packed," Judy's husband, Ray, said as he put his blue nylon wallet back into his pocket.

The couple was dressed in their best clothing—Judy in her sexiest dress and heels and Ray in his polyester blend casual wear from the Sears Men's Store. He had even slicked back his hair, achieving the rarely obtained *perfect comb-over*. Since this was one of the only times his bald pate was completely covered, he had made sure to liberally apply the hairspray before it had fallen. Preservation was the key in a hairdo like his. Judy had gone to the hair dresser earlier that day so she was as equally well-coiffed. They were definitely ready to swing tonight.

"It sure is," Judy nodded.

She was just a little nervous as they walked into the swing club which in previous incarnations had been a restaurant, a doctor's office and a city maintenance facility among other things. Any scrimping on the décor or cleanliness was overlooked due to the fact that swingers are just happy to have a place to do their thing. Even so, the place wasn't half bad.

On the way over in their minivan, Judy couldn't help but rub her pussy just a little. Her mouth was watering just a little bit in anticipation of what was going to happen tonight. She had been looking forward to it all week and now that it was about to happen again, she was almost climbing the walls. She felt extremely sexy in her short, spaghetti strapped dress, *sans underwear.* She never wore panties to the club because she knew that she would just lose them anyway. She remembered one time at the club when a very large black woman wearing nothing but a towel had wandered around the place asking everyone she saw, "Has anybody seen my drawers?"

It had been so embarrassing. She definitely didn't want to be like that woman so she always made a point to leave hers at home.

Money had been a little tight since Ray's hours had been cut at the plant, but this was one expense that she had been disinclined to discard. Besides, Ray still spent money on his stupid SEC football pay-per-view, so she felt more than justified in spending money on going to the swing club. And damn it, this was something she actually needed! She was so wound up with tension most of the time that she had to get it out the best way she knew how. And the swing club just happened to be the best way for her to get unkinked. Ray could always watch whatever was on the networks if he had to. It was a whole lot harder to get gangbanged. Besides it was because of him that she was kinked up to begin with. He just really got on her nerves sometimes.

They were greeted by the staff because they were regulars. "Howdy, Judy," the sleazy, slightly pudgy owner said to her.

She simply detested his greasy, salt and pepper ponytail. She also wasn't very fond of his ever-present velour shirt that he always sported. Unbuttoned to the navel, of course.

He wasn't a bad guy, and did run a good club with a good buffet, at least as far as swing clubs went, but he just got on her nerves. He was always complimenting her on how nice her tits looked or how great her ass was at the most inappropriate times. She had been flattered at first. What woman doesn't love it when a man lusts after her? She knew she was built and loved the fact that her body made men's dicks hard. It was just that he did it at the most awkward times. He never did it when she was turned on and just about to get down to business. He did it when it made no sense to do so. Like when she was in mid-chew of a chocolate covered strawberry.

"Man, Judy, I just get hard thinking about that tight ass of yours. I can't wait to fuck it tonight," he would say.

"Mmmph," she would answer, her mouth full.

Or he would catch her on the way out of the ladies room.

"Man, Judy, those tits of yours are making me have butterflies," he would say and give them a little rub.

She didn't mind his hands on her, because having men grope and touch her was her thing. It was just that she didn't really like it when she was doing something private like using the restroom. Why couldn't he say it when she was in the middle of a circle jerk or when she was sucking a cock? She was a lady after all.

They went to the buffet, got some finger foods and then sat down. She was too excited to eat much because she wanted to get down to business fast. She wasn't one of these women who had to wait around until closing time to get going. She liked to get it on quick. The more the merrier. Quantity was her kink. She had a lot of ground to cover and she wasn't one to waste time. She looked around at who was there.

"I think we're the only couple," Ray said, munching on a spring roll, smacking his lips and licking his fingers. He really enjoyed the buffet, especially the appetizers. It was good that they constituted the majority of the dishes served there.

She winced at how uncouth and ill-mannered he was. This kind of behavior didn't bother her at home but when they were out and about, it really grated on her. It was probably the reason why she was so kinked up all the time.

"I think you're right," she answered, taking a sip of coke.

There was no drinking for her either. She didn't need to be drunk to get going. In fact, she liked to be in complete control of her faculties. It was all about the cock to her. And that was about it. Inebriation was for the women who had to be coaxed into gangbanging. This was definitely not the case for Judy.

She looked around again to confirm what her husband had said and it was true. There were no other females yet except for the girls who worked there. It was all guys. Things were getting off to a good start, all right.

"I love single guy night," she said and got up and walked around the room. What usually scared away most couples from the swing club was what brought her out. While Ray insisted on gorging himself on finger foods, these single guys were going to be her buffet and she was ready to dine.

Ray wolfed down the rest of his spring rolls because he knew that they were about to get started. He got up and followed her around the club. As she walked around from man to man, introducing herself and flirting, Judy was pleased with what she saw. There were black guys, white guys, young guys, old guys, country guys, city guys and just about everybody in between.

The fellows knew what was up and when Ray began to kiss her and feel her up, he told a young, white guy. "C'mon back into the group room. Tell everybody."

He and Judy then went back to the back of the club where the sex rooms were situated. Judy couldn't help but become more and more and turned on, if that were possible.

Judy had never been with any guys other than her husband before she had started doing this, but had always fantasized about being surrounded by good looking men who were all worshipping her and pleasuring her. However, she had never acted upon such a desire, being such a prim and proper woman. In fact, she had never even told anybody about it. And to beat that, she had almost divorced Ray when he had started bringing up the idea of swinging to her.

Sex had never been a big thing with her. It was just something you went through in order to get some sleep. In fact she had rarely orgasmed with Ray. He just wasn't that good, she thought. His idea of sex was to climb on top of her and root around like a hog until he was finished which was usually signified by him grunting like he had finally succeeded in taking a crap. Not very sexy by anyone's definition.

When Ray had first brought up the idea of wife-swapping, she had thought he was a pervert or was just trying to connive a way to have sex with other women. She knew him like a book and in fact she was right. This was what he was doing, but after a while of brow-beating her, she had finally consented to go to a swing club. She had hated it but had reconciled herself that she was going to have to go along if she was to remain married to him. Besides she had found the dressing up and socializing part of it at least somewhat agreeable. That was the only way she had even been able to tolerate it. She figured that it was just a phase that would pass for him. She really didn't want to divorce him even though the thought was somewhat appealing at times.

Eventually, he started hounding her into having sex with a woman. Again, she went through it just to get him to shut up. While it had been nice for him, it had been about as much of a turn on for her as kissing a naugahyde sofa. She just couldn't get into anything.

Then one day while they were at a club—she had again gone just to appease Ray—she had walked by one of the group rooms and had seen a woman in there surrounded by men. It was single guy night, which she had hated because there were very few couples there and every guy there was trying to steamroll her into having sex. In the room the men were groping the woman, fucking her and she was sucking them. It was a gangbang. There had to be at least five of them on her and she was loving every minute. Judy couldn't help but watch and the woman didn't seem to mind. For the first time, Judy had found herself getting extremely turned on and couldn't help but start masturbating while she watched. The sight of the woman getting fucked by all those guys was connecting with something primal in her. This was the first time that this swinger lifestyle had done anything remotely that was a hit with her. And this time it was a homerun. She had previously thought before that swinging was overrated and there wasn't anything to it. Now, she was rethinking it.

After a few minutes of watching the gangbang she had left the room, found Ray and fucked him right there at the club. He was happy but puzzled because she didn't tell him what she had seen. Oddly enough, that was the first time she had really enjoyed sex. Even though it was with Ray.

They soon left the club, but over the next week, she couldn't get the gangbang out of her mind. Her mouth watered at the thought of it and she couldn't help but masturbate constantly. For the first time in her marriage, she couldn't wait to get out of her Sedgefields and into something slinky. More slutty. She knew that she had to go back to the club. Ray was surprised when she said that they were going the next weekend and he was even more surprised when she allowed herself to be gangbanged by six guys. When she orgasmed for the fifth time, she knew that this was it. She was home.

It was at this time that she realized that she loved gangbanging and understood now just what she had been missing from swinging. She had been expecting the champagne and designer lingerie she had seen on the salacious stories about swingers that were always featured on the news magazines. In reality, she had always ended up with the Miller Lite and polyester panties instead. But now she understood. She had been looking for atmosphere, but she had been missing the point. Some girls loved other girls, some girls loved strange, but she loved volume. She loved fucking a mass of guys.

And that's how it had been. While Ray had originally been the person who had wanted to go to the swing club, now it was Judy. He had reluctantly taken a back seat while she screwed. And she did it a lot. She had gotten to the point that she couldn't live without it and every so often, she simply *had* to get her dose of cum. She loved being fucked and it was something that she could now not live without. And now that she was finally getting satisfied sexually, she was a much happier person so her marriage was much more stable. She could definitely tolerate Ray more than she had previously. Having sex with lots of other men made sex with him something she could get through much more easily. He wasn't any better at it, but the idea that there were options other than him made it almost enjoyable.

Ray was into this new lifestyle as well. Or at least he acted like he was. He even helped her set up her gangbangs and acted as security for her to keep any men from getting out of control. While he had originally fantasized about him and Judy having threesomes with other girls, he had been forced to reconcile himself to the fact that this wasn't going to happen that often. If at all. It hadn't yet anyway. Swinging had been his idea after all and he would have to live with the way things were and hope that maybe he would eventually get a shot to do the stuff that he wanted to do. He just hadn't counted on this—a wife that was addicted to cock.

The fact of the matter was that he really didn't have a choice because she had told him that this was how it was going to be regardless if he liked it or not. Besides it was easier for her to do her thing, he had found. A woman who liked to get gangbanged was a hell of a lot more popular than a guy who wanted to screw other men's wives. At least that was his personal experience anyway. Why fight it? It was still a turn on after all.

After Ray had told the young guy to tell everybody to go to the group room, he and Judy had gone there immediately. It was a large space in the back of the swing club that smelled strongly of body odor and consisted of some large mats and a couple of couches and was mercifully dim so that any bad housekeeping was hard to notice. Once they were in it, Judy and Ray started kissing. She ran her fingers though his comb-over. She couldn't but cringe as she felt the spray.

"Careful with the hair, Judy," Ray said. "It took me a long time to get it like this."

Judy took a deep breath and tried to get the feeling of his sprayed hair out of her mind. She eagerly looked over his shoulder and soon was rewarded when the guys started filtering into the room. Ray moved around behind her and she gestured for them to come over. They stood back timidly at first. Ray started feeling her up, rubbing her breasts and moving his hands up and down her body.

"C'mon over guys and get a feel. She likes it."

This was how they usually started. They went in stages. First, Judy liked to get groped and felt up to orgasm. This would make her so horny that she would screw a doorknob. Next she would fuck them all. After that she would suck them to orgasm and let them blast her all over her face and body. This is how they always did it and it never got old for her. She had tried sucking them before fucking them early on in her gangbanging career, but had been disappointed because so many of the men had shot their wads, the number that could screw her had been significantly diminished. She hadn't made that mistake again.

The men came over and started. There had to be at least ten of them tonight. Judy didn't even look at their faces because she didn't care what they looked like. She was just into the sensation. White hands and black hands and brown hands were all over her, rubbing and groping her.

Ray listened for and heard the sound of unzipping and was compelled to tell the men as he usually did, "There's no sex yet. You can stroke it, but nothing more than feeling up now."

He almost had a script at this point. He had to keep the eager beavers at bay otherwise Judy would really let him have it when they got home. Of course the regulars never had to be told to keep it in their pants this early on. They knew what was going to happen tonight. They knew that they would get their turn. In fact, it was probably why they came. Judy was quite well-known for her proclivities in the local swinging community and was considered a guaranteed fuck.

The groping continued after Ray's announcement. Numerous hands were on her pussy and on her tits, rubbing and getting a feel however they could. They even reached around her and rubbed her ass. She moaned and felt the orgasm come up. Her dress by this time was up around her stomach and the top of it was down past her breasts. Ray held her up against the press of flesh and Judy could feel his erection behind her. Men were kissing her on the neck and mouth and she was being overwhelmed with sensation. She could see the owner of the club there too, getting a feel but she didn't mind. She also saw that a couple of women she knew were standing at the door with their husbands and masturbating themselves under their short dresses while they watched her being groped. They had just come into the club. Pheromones were running wild and the smell of sex was strong in the room. The smell of armpits and feet was also quite potent but that was par for the course of such establishment.

This went on for a little while, until Judy had had another couple of orgasms.

"I'm ready for a break," she whispered to Ray.

At that he said loudly, "Okay, everybody off."

He had to say it a couple of more times before it filtered through the men's lust. A couple of minutes later, the men started backing off. The ones that had done this before helped dissipate the crowd and eventually all the men had left.

Judy reached around and kissed Ray squarely on the mouth. The other women walked over to her while she smoothed her dress back down.

"That was almost too much!" one of them wearing a black miniskirt said to her.

"Yeah, I came just from watching it," the other one said. She was wearing a short, tight red dress and stripper heels. "I wish I had the guts to do something like that."

Judy smiled proudly. It always made her feel good when someone was impressed by her sexual appetite. "I'm glad you liked the show. I hope you're going to stick around for the second act."

"I wouldn't miss it for anything," the first one said. At that the three women went to the buffet. Ray stayed around and talked to the women's husbands about football.

Judy munched on some chicken wings and diet coke while she let her lust build again. She didn't have much of an appetite so she chewed the chicken absentmindedly. She was still turned on and knew that it wouldn't be long before she would be climbing the walls again. Pretty soon she was ready and looking around for Ray who was helping himself to the buffet again. A few minutes later, he joined her.

"More spring rolls?" she said a little irritated as he began stuffing her face.

"Mmmph…" he said licking his fingers, completely unaware of her sarcasm.

Judy was even more irritated with him than usual because he was distracting her from thinking about what was going to happen to. She needed to be fucked now and his stomach was the only thing standing in her way.

"How long is it going to take you to eat those damn things?" she snapped.

Ray looked up and hurriedly finished eating the spring rolls.

The woman who was wearing the red dress started laughing, "I think she's ready! Look at her! She's so horny! There's no telling what she'll do if you get between her and a dick!"

Judy laughed nervously and softened a little. Her hormones were raging again and she couldn't even think about laughing. She began to squirm in her seat, crossing and uncrossing her legs. The group grope was just the appetizer and now her sexual hunger was overpowering. She leaned over and kissed Ray on the neck and he kissed her back, rubbing her big tits.

"I didn't mean to snap, I'm just ready to get going."

They got up and the regulars alerted the other guys as to what was going on. Soon, they were in the group room again. Judy was already on her knees and had her dress up and was fingering herself when they started streaming in. There were more now than there had been earlier in the evening. There were some new ones this time that hadn't been in the club earlier. She was hungrily giving Ray a blowjob when the guys started lining up and standing in a circle around her. There had to be at least fifteen this time, including the women's husbands. The women had come into the room and were lustily pawing at each other while they watched from a couch.

After tasting Ray's precum, she went from guy to guy, bringing each almost to the point of orgasm before backing off. She sucked and deep-throated and when she felt them begin to tense or tasted the impending climax, she would

64

stop. She was pleased at how well-hung the turnout was. She was going to be sore in the morning, she thought gleefully. She was going to be worked like a borrowed mule.

After she had gotten them all up and to the brink, she got down on the mat and lay on her back. She was going to be flatbacking straight up and she wanted a look at each one of the men who was going to fuck her. She wasn't really concerned about their faces, but wanted to see their cocks and skin color. She, of course, let Ray go first because after all, they were married and it was the right thing to do, regardless of whether she really wanted to screw him or not. When he was about to cum, he moved over to her mouth. She sucked him until he came all over her face.

It was after that that it officially started, man after man fucking her. They would come at her two at a time, each one penetrating her pussy and riding her hard while she ground back. She would fuck one and suck another one, each taking his turn until both had fucked her. She would then let them cum all over face and tits.

The first guy was a tall, white, trashy looking skinny guy she hadn't seen before. He was covered in jailhouse tattoos and was hung too, probably the biggest guy there. She knew that she would get her good and opened up for the rest and he did, ramming her good and making her cum.

"Fuck me trailer park style, you fucking jailbird," she said as he had nailed her. He gave a primal grunt as a response.

A big Cuban with a fat dick fucked her next and his dick made her want to scream.

"Give it to me hard, you panini-dicked fucker," she said as he pounded her.

He had a hard time not laughing at this. He stepped up the pace and the next sound out of her mouth was an orgasmic scream.

And that's the way it was. It was like each dick was filling up a space the previous one hadn't. It was like they were connecting the dots. One would be wide; the next one would be long. It was like every square bit of her pussy was being occupied at one point or another. Each guy came a lot and was she was quickly getting coated. She didn't care because she was getting the cock she needed. She would feel the orgasms coming in waves and with each thrust of the well-hung studs, her ecstasy grew. She was orgasming faster than usual but was in no danger of being finished. All of the men were larger than average so they were the perfect size for her, filling her up and wearing her out.

Soon she wanted it doggie style and stood up, stretching her legs. A skinny black guy who was a regular was up next.

"Grab them ankles gal!" he yelled, shaking his head and bugging out his eyes like he was going insane. His erection was so large and so hard it seemed to almost be lifting his thin body off the ground.

She smiled and clapped her hands and grabbed her ankles and bent over for him. He was one of her favorites because he had a good personality and was hung like a horse. He stuck it in and started pounding her. She moaned when the cocks began penetrating her more deeply. She orgasmed shortly after he started.

She turned back around to give the next one full access to her pussy. Suddenly, she had new sensation. Sure she was getting fucked, but it was different. More intense, yet there was different vibe going on. She saw that it was a little person who taking a turn at her. He was what some people would refer to as a dwarf. And he was really going at it.

A big country guy who had came on her earlier started laughing. "Look at that little feller! If he told her to grab grass, he'd have to get a bucket to stand on! Hee Haw!"

Judy had never really liked this guy because he had once asked Ray to hold his underwear (he referred to them as his *step-ins*) while he was having sex with her. The only reason she tolerated him because he was a pretty good screw.

The little person grinned and flipped the country guy off.

"I'll get you a bucket because I definitely want to grab some grass," Judy said smiling and rubbing her clit with two fingers. "

"Then start grabbin'!" he said and started pounding her even harder, taking her breath away. It was probably the most extreme fucking she had gotten all evening and she came effortlessly.

After he finished, she got down on her hands and knees and took on the rest of the crowd. She orgasmed again and again and soon felt limp from all the pleasure that she was experiencing. The more she fucked, the more she could feel herself relaxing and soon could feel herself leveling back out again.

Meanwhile, the two women were eating each other out while they watched her being nailed. Some clueless single guys who had been standing in line for Judy were hovering around them, hoping for a turn, but these two girls were strictly into each other and no men were invited. Except to watch, that is.

Soon she had worked her way through every man willing to gangbang her and she was covered in cum. The last guy had blasted the biggest load she had ever seen all over tits which were now dripping semen down her stomach and onto her pussy. She looked over at Ray who grinning from ear to ear. Sprigs of his hair had fallen gently onto his forehead. His hairspray had yielded earlier in the evening so his combover had been unleashed and was developing a mind of its own.

"Man!" he said. "You really turned it loose, tonight!"

"Did I?" Judy said and smiled. "I think I'm unkinked now."

"I would hope so," he laughed. "Who wouldn't be after that?"

"I know I sure had fun," she said. She looked down at her dress and thought about putting it back on, but decided not to just yet. "I'm hungry, let's get something off the buffet," she said. She knew now that she would at least be able to tolerate Ray and his uncouth eating habits a little better.

"Okay," he said

After Judy had showered, they walked out and to the buffet. She was feeling pleased with herself because she had gotten what she needed. Ray immediately went and filled his plate with spring rolls. He started eating them even before he made it back to the table. Even though she was unkinked, Judy couldn't help but wince

They ate and chatted with some people and then Judy got dressed and they went back to their minivan and drove home. After they had been on the road a couple of minutes, Ray began fumbling around in his pocket.

"What are you doing?" Judy asked, thinking his behavior quite odd. "Did you lose your phone?"

"No. I was just craving a spring roll. I took some from the buffet," he said producing some of the Asian appetizer wrapped up in a greasy napkin. "Do you want one?"

Judy took a deep breath and shook her head. Ray shrugged and began eating. His comb-over flopped as he chewed enthusiastically.

She closed her eyes. She couldn't believe it. It had just been a few minutes since she had gotten gangfucked and he was already getting on her nerves. She began to feel that nervous feeling again. That aching need to do something to

68

alleviate the tension. It was just like craving a cigarette. The sight of Ray with his comb-over and eating spring rolls had kinked her up again and the effect had almost been instant.

"Ray, I think we're going to have to go back tomorrow. I don't think I got it worked out tonight."

He shook his head and laughed. "Sure thing," he said automatically. He knew she needed it and if she didn't get it she would make his life hell.

She began fingering herself. Even after all that, she still wanted more. And she knew deep down that she would never get her fill. Especially as long as she was married to Ray. There would never be enough cock for her, even if it was stretched from here to the moon. She smiled with the anticipation. You see, some people might call it a sickness, this addiction to cock that Judy had. But she didn't. It was just something that was a necessary part of her married life just like cooking or paying the bills. The exception being that it was a lot more fun than any of the other stuff she had to do.

Ray, of course, was looking forward to the spring rolls. And other finger foods.

The Bitch in the Basement

"Fuck me, you cunt!" she yelled throatily as she urged her gym rat girlfriend on.

Her girlfriend plowed into her even harder with the strap-on. That thing was huge, too. She had an intense look of concentration as she ground against the big black rubber dildo. Thrusting hard with her muscular legs, she turned and hungrily licked the huge dick in front of her. She groaned as she took a breath and deep-throated it, temporarily consuming all the meat of the hung stud. She held onto his ass with both of her strong hands as she went up and down on his cock. She was literally insatiable because all the while, she kept fucking, never missing a beat with her girlfriend. Her big breasts swung in time as she got jackhammered.

"I'm going to cum!" her girlfriend said as she kept pumping with the dildo, the base of it rubbing against her pussy. She shuddered as the climax hit her. Her muscles shimmered from the perspiration she had worked up.

"Let's switch, I need the real thing now," she said breathlessly and got down on her back on the sofa.

Her girlfriend then straddled her face as the dude went balls deep in, pounding her. Her face was wet with pussy as she munched on her girlfriend's snatch, her powerful arms rubbing her big tits.

Master Donald fought the urge to masturbate as he secretly stood at the top of the stairs leading to the basement listening to the sounds of sex. He had to be quiet or she would become angry. But she was so hot, with her white hair and gorgeous, muscled body that it was hard not to just whip it out and start beating it. And she knew how to fuck and control every sexual situation. This combined with the fact that she was a bottomless pit when it came to dick and pussy made keeping his hands off himself even harder.

"Fuck me harder, you stupid bastard!" she yelled at the guy as she looked up from the pussy she was eating. Her big jugs heaved up and down as she fucked and when the other girl started humping her face with orgasm, she really began to squirm.

Then it was time for her to cum. She screamed as she convulsed and spasmed. The guy pulled out and blasted all over her tits. Both she and her girlfriend licked it up and cleaned him off, eating the entire creamy load. He stood over them with a smug yet dumb look on his face.

"Now get over there and sit down until we need you again," she barked at him and started making out with her girlfriend.

He obeyed and sat down in the dingy armchair. The semen swapped between both the women's mouths as they kissed. Now they were really turned on and began to scissor each other with their well-developed legs, grinding their pussies against each other. She had a concentrated crazy look in her eyes as she and her girlfriend looked intensely at each other. They both howled as they came again.

With that Master Donald scurried back up the steps of the basement and hurried into the kitchen. He knew that he had better get started on lunch. He knew that after all the fucking she had been doing that morning she would ravenous. She was always hungry anyway due to the fact she worked out all the time, but was especially famished after fucking.

In other words he had better start hopping if he didn't want her to lose her temper.

"Donald! If you don't get your ass back down here with our sandwiches, I'm really going to beat the hell out of you. And this time you definitely *won't* like it!" she yelled from down in the basement a few minutes later as he hurried around the kitchen, rushing to gather the ingredients for the roast beef, tomato and cheese sandwiches.

"And you better cut the crusts off it this time, you dildo!"

Master Donald winced because he shuddered at what had happened the last time he had forgotten. "Don't forget to cut the crust. Don't forget to cut the crust," he muttered over and over to himself so that he wouldn't forget.

Sometimes he felt foolish, completely catering to this woman. But he knew that he didn't have a choice. If he didn't do what she wanted, she just wouldn't shut up. She would keep on and on until he gave in.

And then there would be the punishment. He trembled at this thought and picked up the pace.

He looked down at himself and realized that most of his friends and accounting colleagues would think he looked ridiculous in his leather outfit and hood. He was middle-aged, dumpy, hairy, short, dressed in bondage gear. He knew that any credibility he had would be gone in an instant if they ever saw his get-up. However, he didn't care. At least not when he was at home. This was who he really was. He was Master Donald, damn it. Before she had shown up, he had fancied himself a Dominant. A slave master. A sadist. He was the one who administered the punishment. He was the one in charge.

But now he no longer had such fantasies. He knew that he was in charge of nothing. He just wanted to appease her. He just wanted to shut her up. It was hard to even think of himself as Master Donald anymore. Most of the time now, he was just Donald. Or whatever insulting term she saw fit to refer to him as.

"No scratch that, calling you a dildo is an insult to dildos. I actually like dildos. Dildos are useful. And we know that you're absolutely useless, you hairy fuck!"

There was laughter from her girlfriend and the dude.

He kept his head down and kept making the sandwiches, trying not to let her insults get to him. He couldn't afford to make a mistake on the sandwich.

"And don't get any body hair in our food, you sawed-off Sasquatch!" she yelled again making the others laugh. "You're so hairy you're just like a big pussy. Maybe we should just fold you up and fuck you!" She added, "If you weren't so damned dirty."

"Maybe he should get his body shampooed," her girlfriend added, cackling.

"Shampooed? Hell, he's so hairy, he can't even take a bath. He has to be dipped!"

The others laughed even harder which encouraged her further.

"The only other way he can get clean is to vacuum himself!" she added, horselaughing.

This got an even bigger laugh out of everyone.

Master Donald grimaced but kept working. That wasn't true. He had never had to vacuum himself. He couldn't believe how much abuse he was taking from her. It really was pathetic that he actually used to think he was in control.

He stopped for a second and listened.

There was some movement near the steps! Was she coming up here to check on him?! He hoped not. He needed her to stay down there. In the basement.

Most men would have begged her to come up and see them. She was beautiful with her Nordic looks and muscular yet feminine body. She had to be over six feet tall and built with bleached white hair. She was enough to make a man just whip it out and start jerking it just from looking at her. Her tits alone were enough to cause mass erections, but the fact that she dressed in that tiny leather sling bikini and boots—when she wore anything—was enough to make a man salivate. Especially a man like Master Donald. Even though, she was easy on his eyes, she was absolute hell on his nerves. In fact, she just grated on him. If she hadn't walked around nude most of the time, he really wouldn't have been able to stand her. He listened again. The movement on the steps was only in his imagination. He breathed a sigh of relief.

As he continued to make the sandwiches, taking his time so that he didn't make a mistake, he thought back over how he had ended up in this position. How he had wound up essentially being a flunky to this platinum goddess. It wasn't supposed to be this way. This wasn't what he had wanted when he had contacted her.

But how had everything gone so wrong?

A few months earlier, Master Donald had finally made the first step in making his BDSM fantasies a reality. He had placed an ad on the internet about how he wanted a submissive.

He had been looking at the BDSM websites and attending the bondage clubs for a while before deciding to place the ad. He had a rather large home that he had bought from his parents a few years earlier. It was a rancher and was situated out by itself in an older community in the suburbs so any screams or yells would most likely not be heard by the neighbors. And it had a fully furnished basement. Sure the décor was circa 1979, but it made a pretty good dungeon if one ignored the shag carpet and crappy furniture. It had been his hangout until his parents had moved to Florida. It was at that point that he had graduated up to the ground floor and converted the basement into his makeshift torture chamber. He had fitted it with some bondage gear and other assorted equipment and was absolutely itching to try it out on someone other than himself.

After he had started his search on the internet, it had taken about a week before he had settled on her, the one in the basement now. None of the rest of the other women had felt right, he had told himself after the fact. But in actuality, he had chosen her because she was a knockout. She was also local. He wouldn't have to pay for her bus ticket or anything. This was very attractive to the accountant in him.

Most importantly, though, she had sent a nude photo of herself.

He had responded favorably to her email (and photo) and invited her over. He was overjoyed that she accepted. She was going to come over the following Friday. Punishing her was going to be a pleasure and he could hardly wait. She was so beautiful and muscular, she looked like a character from the comic books that he enjoyed so much. He couldn't wait to degrade her. He was going to whip her with his cat of nine tails. He was going to flog her. He was going to make her do all sorts of sexual things to him. He was going to use her and he was going to make sure she loved it. He even had a contract ready for her to sign designating her as his slave. She hadn't said anything about her experience, but he vowed that she was going to worship him by the time it was over.

He had been so excited that he could barely make it through the week and was pleased when the doorbell rang thirty minutes early that Friday. He was already wearing his hood and leather when he opened the door.

"Come in, slave," he said in his most authoritative voice. He tried to be impressive and commanding, but when he saw her, he almost instantly shrank. She was that imposing.

"Here, carry these," she said casually and handed him her suitcases.

He took them without thinking. She was wearing a black leather trench coat and black boots. Even covered up, he could tell that she was very well-built and muscular. Her picture hadn't lied. She definitely looked like she worked out a lot. She was also smoking a cigarette and drinking a Michelob. She walked on in like she owned the place.

Hmm...what the hell is in these things? Master Donald thought as he struggled with her bags. While she had handled them like they were nothing, he was having a hard time picking them up.

"There was no need for you to bring any bondage gear, I have plenty," Master Donald said, trying to regain control of the situation. "Also I don't allow smoking in the house. So if you don't mind..."

"What?" she asked absentmindedly, then gestured at the luggage. "Oh, yeah, right...whatever...put them in the spare bedroom." She continued to smoke.

"What?" Master Donald asked incredulously. Something was wrong here. She had yet to ask his permission for anything. She was supposed to be a submissive. She wasn't supposed to be ordering him around. And she had disobeyed him in regards to her smoking. How dare she!

"I said, put them in the spare bedroom," she ordered and took off the trench coat. From her tone, it was very clear that he didn't have an option to do anything but.

When the coat came off, he could see that she was wearing a slinky black dress underneath. It was quite obvious that she wasn't wearing any underwear because when she stood a certain way, you could see through it. Besides it just barely covered her nipples. It accentuated her prodigious curves and muscles nicely. He also couldn't help but notice her strong, muscular legs. She looked like she could break a man in half with those things. Later on, he noted when she would wear her sling bikini and boots, she really did look like a superhero in her get-up, unlike Master Donald with his leather hood, who looked like an absolute fool.

"Don't you understand English?" she asked narrowing her ice blue eyes at him.

"Oh, I do. I just didn't realize that you were going to be staying."

She gave him an eat shit look and lit another cigarette. Now, it was obvious that she had no intention of honoring his non-smoking policy.

Oh well, maybe we'll really be able to get into some role playing, Master Donald thought hopefully, deciding on second thought not to push the non-smoking thing. He didn't want to be a bad host after all.

"How about the basement?" he suggested. "It's furnished. In fact it's kind of like an apartment. It's probably okay for you to smoke down there. I don't think it'll bother me that much."

"Great," she mumbled under her breath and took a swig of beer. "Then take my suitcases down there." She exhaled smoke directly in his face.

"Okay," Master Donald said politely, trying not to cough. He turned as he started towards the basement. "When do you want to get started?" he asked eagerly, trying his best to be casual.

She narrowed her eyes. "Started? Started on what?

"You know the BDSM stuff. When do you want me to get started punishing you? I know you've been bad," he sniveled and snorted. "How about I teach you a lesson about smoking in the house?" he snorted again. Maybe it was a little forward of him saying this, but he was the dominant after all.

"BDS-what?" she asked then realized what he was talking about. "Oh, yeah, that. How about this, why don't you give it a rest for a second and go do what I told you."

He looked at her curiously. Then she opened her legs just a little so he could see her shaved pussy.

"Okay, then there's no hurry. We'll get it into later," he said, blushing, and hurried down the stairs.

"That's what I thought," she said contemptuously. "And don't go through my panties either, you pervert."

What a joke, he bitterly thought later. She didn't even have any panties.

And that's how it started. Him bustling and doing stuff for her while she insulted him.

Regardless of her admonishment not to, he had taken the liberty of looking through her suitcase to see what kind of stuff she was into it. It was his house after all. He was a little surprised when he didn't find nothing but sling bikinis, slutty dresses, dumbbells and stripper shoes. And the biggest vibrators and dildos he had ever seen. This stuck him as puzzling coming from a person who had answered a BDSM personal ad. There was nothing BDSM related of any sort whatsoever. He just couldn't understand this. But later he found out the reason. And it didn't take a rocket scientist to figure it out.

The fact was that she wasn't even into BDSM. She had just need a place to crash and had answered his ad because she had smelled a mark. She was looking for a person to freeload off and had sensed that Master Donald would be an easy take.

He had begun to realize this later that night when she again refused to let him punish her. It was right after he had just ordered take-out from a Chinese place up on the main road. She had asked him if she minded if she took off her clothes. He had taken this to mean that she was finally going to open up and submit herself to him. That was when he had suggested it—the punishing. And when he had found out the truth.

"You beat me?" She laughed. "You're kidding, right?"

In the nude she was even more intimidating than when she was in her clothes. He couldn't stop looking at her breasts and muscular tanned body. If he didn't know better, he would have thought she knew what she was doing to him. Bullying him.

"Well, if you're backing out of the arrangement, then you need to leave," Master Donald said, mustering up every bit of his strength. He was going to show her who was boss. He wasn't going to take this kind of disrespect from anyone. "I have very definite requirements in a submissive and if you're not willing to submit then you need to go on your way."

"I don't think so, pudgy," she said smirking and produced his address book which he had carelessly left lying about. "You kick me out or call the police, I'm going to call everyone in this book and tell them about your little secret fantasy world. Some people don't care what other people think about them, but somehow I don't think you're one of them."

Master Donald gulped. For a second, he had thought that he may have been mistaken and had clicked the box requesting a dominant instead of a submissive. At least she was into at least some aspect of the BDSM lifestyle, he thought desperately. At least maybe they would have that in common.

But alas, he eventually realized that he was mistaken about this as well.

She wasn't even trying to be dominant, even though she was very physically and mentally dominating. She was just a generally disagreeable, obnoxious, unpleasant person who thought nothing of intimidating and marginalizing him. And took every opportunity to do so just so she would have a free place to live. Besides that, she was usually drunk which only served to make her behavior even more intolerable.

"And, as far as someone being someone's slave, I think you know how that's going to work out," she leaned over and pushed her long manicured nail into his soft stomach. "Now get me a Michelob. I'm thirsty."

"But I don't have any," he whimpered, not quite knowing what to do.

"Well go buy some," she roared. "They're not just going to grow feet and walk here on their own, you stupid bastard!"

As time progressed, she began to bring over her girlfriends. And loads of men. She would have sex all the time, flaunting her well-built perfect muscular body in front of Master Donald. Torturing him. From the looks of some of the sleazes she brought in. she would fuck anything that moved. Who knew where she found these guys? It seemed that the only prerequisite was that they had to be hung. It didn't matter if they were black, white or purple, she would fuck anybody if he had a big dick. Or a pussy.

Naturally, of course, this left out Master Donald. He was hung like a bird. What was most insulting was that she didn't even bother to check to see if he was packing. She just *knew.* And she made the most of the fact that he had so much to hide in regards to his BDSM lifestyle.

After she had produced his address book, he knew that there was really nothing he could do. He had too much to lose. He was in a leadership position at work and there was no way he could lose that. He didn't have that much going on career-wise other than his accounting job and he was too old to start over. He realized that he would just have to put up with her until he figured something out. At least she was good to look at.

Despite this, after a while the fact that she was bringing people over to fuck began to really irritate him. He didn't mind the orgy action going on in his house, but the fact that she never let him join? Now that bugged him. He could let the BDSM stuff go, but he was still a man after all. Eventually one evening, he had had enough.

He had listened for about hour to the howls of pleasure coming from the basement. She had invited three guys over to gangbang her while one of her girlfriends videotaped it. She sold sex tapes of herself at the flea market to make beer and cigarette money. Of course, she didn't share any of the money with him, he thought bitterly. Or offer him any beer or cigarettes. Even though he didn't even smoke, the slight was not lost on him.

He had listened at the top of the stairs, stroking his cock, aching for some action and finally decided that if she was going to blackmail him out of free room and board, the least he could get was a fuck out of the deal. He put on his hood and pounded down the steps.

She was on a mat on the floor astride on big black guy while sucking and giving hand jobs to two other sleazy white guys. The guys were so big and muscular that they made her look normal-sized. Also, their dicks were proportionate to their bodies which meant they were huge. Master Donald was a little intimidated because he was so small but he was horny as hell so he didn't care. Her girlfriend shot him a mean look and stepped aside so that he didn't get in the shot. She had one hand on her pussy and the other on the camera.

Master Donald stepped up to her in mid-moan as she thrusted against the stud she was sitting on. Her leg muscles rippled as she propelled herself towards orgasm. The guys looked at him like he was an alien or something.

"I'm ready for my turn," he said matter of factly. He whipped his small erection out of his leather pants.

She kept fucking and turned her head from the dick she was sucking. She kept stroking the other two with her hands, her muscular arms really working their cocks. Finally, she noticed him.

"What?" she said distractedly. She was in the middle of deep pleasure. Her large breasts were bouncing up and down as she rode.

"I want to fuck you," he said. "You're living here rent free and it's time that you settle up."

She kept fucking and then it hit her. She knew what he wanted. She smiled. "Of course you do. But there's no way you're coming near me with that little thing."

The guys laughed, but Master Donald was undaunted.

"I don't care. You owe me," he said.

She groaned as the black dick she was riding hit her g-spot. Then she turned back to him. "I've got an idea." She looked to her girlfriend. "Get me the strap-on."

The girlfriend snickered and reached and got the huge strap-on that was lying on the couch.

Master Donald took one look at the strap-on. "Oh no. You're not going to use that thing on me!"

She laughed. "I'm not going to use it on you. You would probably like it too much. Besides the view of your furry back would probably make me lose my lunch. No, you're going to use it on me."

"But...I'm a man," Master Donald protested. "I don't need..."

"Unless you wear it, you're not going to get near me," she said. "I've got to feel what I'm fucking and this is the only way you're going to come close to filling me up."

Master Donald was dumbfounded. Never before had he been so humiliated. He didn't know what to do.

"You do want to fuck me, right?" she said and winced as the stud hit her g-spot again. She licked her lips.

At that Master Donald pulled down his pants and put on the strap-on.

"Okay then," she smiled. She turned to her girlfriend. "Make sure you get this on tape." Her girlfriend smiled back wickedly.

It was after that she kicked it into gear and started riding the black stud she was on, quickly reaching orgasm. Her muscles flexed and glistened as she worked up a sweat. She then got on all fours and one of the other guys started pounding. She eagerly started sucking on the black cock.

"This thing tastes even better after it's been inside me," she moaned as she fucked. She ground against the big dick that was fucking her.

Master Donald stood by stroking himself, the big strap-on flopping. He looked ridiculous. He didn't care. He was so turned on, he would have done anything just to be near her.

After a while of fucking the dude, she orgasmed again. She switched to the next one and thrust her pussy against him like she was the one with a dick. He didn't look like he was holding up too well so she went ahead and came.

"Now, come over here, you worm. At least I don't have to worry about you shooting your wad too quick," she said and pulled Master Donald over behind her.

She rammed the dildo into her and began to grind against Master Donald. She was so powerful that her grinding against him almost knocked him down. His hard-on brushed against the back of her powerful leg as she rode the black rubber. It wasn't long before he began to cum and when she felt the ejaculation, she moaned with orgasm and pushed him away. She got on her back and began rubbing her snatch and quickly squirted all over him. She must have had a gallon of fluid because he was drenched. She signaled the other guys over and she lustily began sucking them until they all came all over her.

"Now, leave," she said to Master Donald.

He stood there with a grin on his face. He had never been squirted on before. Even though he had been completely humiliated, he had actually had a pretty good time.

Sensing this, she quickly threw figurative cold water on him.

"Now treasure this, you worthless hairy fuck. This will be the only time you even come close to this," she gestured to her body. "And remember, in case you get any bright ideas about anything, we've got this whole thing on tape," she said wickedly, letting him know that she had yet another way to blackmail him.

He hadn't believed her at first. But when she kicked him in the nuts and told him to get the hell back up the stairs and fix her something to eat, he knew that she wasn't kidding. Her girlfriend and the guys had laughed at him as he had run back up the stairs.

That was the last time he had stood up to her. It was easier just to give in. She would taunt him by masturbating with her big glass dildo in front of him, telling him that he would never be able to touch her body ever again. She would also go on and on about how useless and creepy he was. She had him so beaten down that when she started running up his credit cards buying trashy lingerie, protein powder and workout equipment online, he didn't even protest. He just paid the bill. He just didn't know what to do.

Suddenly his thoughts were interrupted.

"What the hell's taking so long?!" she yelled. "Are you making them with your feet or something?! We want our fucking sandwiches!"

"I'm coming," Master Donald yelled back as he finished the sandwiches. He placed the meal on a tray and prepared to take it down to them. He became erect at the idea of seeing her muscled body and the hope that she would like the sandwich. He didn't care it the others liked it or not. Just so long as she was pleased.

No, this wasn't what he had originally wanted. But since he didn't know what to do about the situation, he figured that he would just live with it. Besides, in a weird way, he was even beginning to enjoy it.

He started down the stairs with the sandwiches. Yes, as long as he could please her, he would be alright. But then again, he realized that it might be even better if he didn't.

Slave Ship

Wendy had been brought up too well to end up so dirty. She hadn't intended for anything like this to happen or hadn't even thought such a thing possible. But sometimes circumstances bring about a situation that is so out of the ordinary that it's inevitable that it will happen to somebody. And this time that somebody just happened to be her.

Two months earlier, Wendy and her friend, Susie, were driving down I-95 to Florida in Susie's Chevy Cavalier. The two secretaries had been saving for months for a vacation and had finally scraped up enough for a Caribbean cruise. They were both young women in their mid-twenties and were looking to find a little adventure and possibly Mister Right. They had met two years earlier and had been friends ever since.

Because their jobs paid next to nothing, their resources were limited, but eventually Wendy had been able to find a vacation they could afford online. She had never heard of the cruise line, but it looked pretty clean and had some decent reviews. It was also supposed to cater to adult singles.

This was a bonus. She had pre-registered with the cruise line, submitting her passport information online. Since it was a singles cruise, she had thought nothing about the cruise line's request to submit a full body shot. However, she had been a little bit uncomfortable about the questionnaire regarding her sexual preferences.

While she had dated a lot in college, she was not what anyone would call a slut. At least not by today's standards. She was proud of the fact that she didn't sleep around with just everybody. She was a good girl, or at least that's the way she thought of herself. She was small-town Americana through and through. But this was largely due to her mother's rigid views regarding sexuality.

"Everybody will talk about you!" That's what her mother had said regarding the subject of sex.

In other words, girls who weren't virtuous were choice subjects of gossip in towns such as hers. In her mother's world view, it was not proper to be talked about and she was going to do everything in her power to dissuade her daughter from being such a girl.

And such admonishments had worked. The auburn-haired Wendy had remained quite chaste. However, while she had been raised to stay a virgin until she was married, that kind of thinking was a little too old-fashioned for her taste. But that was not to say that she didn't have standards. She had at least liked the two guys with whom she had had sex.

Susie, however, wasn't so selective. It almost seemed like she got it on with someone different every week. If it had a pulse and she was in the mood, she would fuck it. It didn't matter if it was male, female, shemale or what. She was just a horny, dirty girl. She figured that if she screwed enough people, she would eventually luck up on a rich man. A rich man that she could tolerate. This would be her road to the easy life as she perceived it. It was a crap shoot she took every weekend. It was amazing that the two girls could be so different sexually and still be such good friends.

"Maybe we'll meet some rich businessmen," Susie said, flicking her dark hair, as they crossed the Florida state line.

"Maybe," Wendy answered.

She had always considered Susie a bit of a gold-digger just because of the way she seemed to seek out certain kinds of men. Susie would screw anyone, but dating long-term was a different thing entirely. If he didn't have a fat wallet, he wouldn't make the cut past the first screw. Unless he was really hung, of course, but even then she would just keep him around for *good times*. It wouldn't ever get any more serious than that.

While Wendy thought such behavior a little unseemly, she really didn't have that much of a problem with it, as long as people didn't associate that kind of conduct with her. She always rolled her eyes whenever Susie bent over and showed her ass or tits in front of the bosses at work. That girl was definitely not afraid to work it to get what she wanted. Regardless if the bosses were single or not.

After they made it to Florida, they quickly found their cruise ship terminal and then located a cheap motel nearby. They figured that they would go out on the town that night and then be ready to board the following morning. They were supposed to be on the ship at eleven o'clock so they had plenty of time. They settled into the room, showered and put on some hot outfits and were ready to hit the town.

Since the cruise ship terminals and, thusly the motel, were nowhere near anything other than old warehouses and other industrial facilities, they had to drive back into town to find the bars.

After driving around for about a half-hour, they finally found some real hopping ones near the university. They were fairly packed, which was something considering it was a Thursday. Studying apparently wasn't that important down here. It was hard not to notice how body conscious everyone was. Most of the women were smoking hot as were the men. Form-fitting and revealing clothes were the norm.

It would have been easy to get caught up in the loud music and party atmosphere had Wendy not restrained herself. The drinks were flowing and the sexual energy was palpable. Wendy allowed herself to drink a little, but kept herself from doing anything other than dancing with a swarthy bodybuilder. She didn't want to get anything going too early into their vacation. She knew they still had a cruise to go on. Besides, she thought his face was too goofy looking to go much farther than that. She didn't think she would be able to do anything too hot and heavy without looking at his face and laughing. He was just that cartoonish looking. Besides, she just wasn't the kind of girl to do anything more than that anyway.

Susie, however, didn't exercise such control. She turned it loose and was partying to beat the band. After about an hour, Wendy found her in the ladies room bent over the sink with a blonde surfer dude balls deep in her pussy. Her big tits were hanging out of the top of her dress, swinging in time to the screwing. She was drunk and oblivious to the other people in the bath room.

"You fucker!" she roared as he pounded her. "Fuck me like a man!"

He got a perplexed look on his face, but he did as she requested, ramming her so hard that he was almost knocking her head into the mirror. She groaned with approval and it was obvious that he was hitting her g-spot. It wasn't long before she came. She soon started screaming and writhing while she climaxed. He waited until she was finished and then came. Hard. He held her big tits as he ejaculated. When he had finished, she turned around and slapped his face.

"What's that for?" he asked, not just a little surprised.

Thanks to the tequila he was drunk on, it was one of his better performances. Considering how hot she was, the fact that he had been able to hold it until she came was quite an achievement for him.

"I wasn't done, yet, you fuckwad," she slurred.

"But you came," he protested.

"I wanted more than one!"

"I can try again," he offered.

Susie smiled a tightlipped smile that let him know that his time with her was truly finished. "No, I'm over it now. Besides, I think I need some pussy."

She looked around the restroom for some likely candidates but apparently wasn't able to find what she was looking for. She went over to Wendy—who had early in their friendship made it clear that girl/girl sex wasn't her thing—and grabbed her arm. "C'mon, let's go," she said.

Wendy was relieved because this was one time she wasn't going to have to force Susie into the car after leaving a bar. Regardless, She couldn't help but be more than little turned on from watching Susie's performance. Seeing how hard she had orgasmed had made her want to rub herself, but she kept from it. She didn't really want to do that here. Not now. It just wasn't a proper thing to do and besides, it was time to get back to the motel. She also didn't want to give Susie a chance to change her mind.

The next morning, due to being out so late the previous night, Wendy and Susie slept later than they had intended and left the motel in much more of a hurry and state of dishevelment than they would have otherwise. They were barely able to get their car parked and dash to the terminal before it was too late.

"Man, I didn't plan on sleeping that late," Wendy said as she hurried into line.

There were still quite a few people who hadn't boarded yet so apparently it wasn't just them who were late. However, they were the very last ones in line.

"Yeah, but I didn't plan on fucking that guy last night either," Susie replied. "But you know how it is when the opportunity presents itself."

"It presents itself to you quite a lot," Wendy said, laughing.

"Jealous!" Susie said and snickered.

Wendy rolled her eyes. "It looks like we're going to be okay though," she said.

"Whew!" Susie said.

They had checked their bags when they had come in so they were now carrying nothing but their purses.

As they stood in line, Wendy thought about the night before at the club and couldn't help but look over at Susie with amusement, envy and just a little disgust.

"You were really out of control last night, you know that?"

Susie smiled. "So?"

Wendy shook her head. "I could never do that sort of thing."

Susie laughed. "You would be better off if you did. No, I wasn't out of control. I'm just an independent woman. I fuck who I feel like fucking."

"Well, no one can accuse you of doing any differently."

The two young women made their way up to the counter where they presented their boarding passes to the clerk, a tall, stern blonde well-built woman in her mid-thirties. From her accent she seemed to be from Scandinavia or somewhere like Scandinavia. Her name tag read, *Inga*. From her demeanor and bearing, it was obvious that this woman, while being extremely good looking, didn't tolerate much nonsense.

"Mmmm...," she said as looked over their paperwork.

They could tell from the way she was looking from her computer to them and then back again that she was looking at the full body pics they had sent of themselves.

"Is there anything wrong?" Susie asked.

"I'm not sure...mmmm," she said.

She picked up the phone and said something in a foreign language. She nodded and said something else that they couldn't understand. She hung up the phone and turned to the girls and smiled coldly. "Everything is good. I had to make sure there wasn't a how you say, glitch, in the software." She laughed.

Susie and Wendy fake laughed out of politeness.

"So, Inga, can we go on through?" Susie asked. They were getting impatient to board.

Inga seemed to bristle at this question. She obviously wasn't too keen on the passengers being so familiar with her, but she didn't say anything. She forced a smile.

"Oh yes. In fact, I'll go with you. You're the very last customers and I'll walk you through myself. You know, give you the tour. Just give me a moment to close up my computer."

"Okay, Inga," the two girls said.

Inga winced a little bit again.

After a moment, she had closed up her computer and took Susie gently by the arm.

"Come with me. You're so lucky, girls. It's so rare that passengers get a tour like this. Usually we just herd you in like cattle and then turn you loose on the buffets so you can eat like pigs."

Then she laughed and they began to walk around and through the ramp up into the boat.

Susie couldn't help but observe how stacked Inga was. She was an Amazon with enormous tits, small waist and perfect ass. Her dark military-inspired uniform really accentuated her body. Her high black boots made her look even taller than she was. Susie couldn't help but feel a little tingle as they walked. Inga was one sexy woman.

They walked up the ramp and into the ship. Wendy and Susie were excited as they looked around the atrium and saw all the other passengers milling about. It was quite a festive environment. The ship was done up in the typical casino-lite décor that is de rigueur of cruise ships of the modern era. The European style fixtures were the only thing to suggest that they weren't in a Native American gaming establishment in upstate New York.

"Wow, this place is nice," Wendy said as she looked around at the gaudily decorated ship.

"Yes, *King Oscar's Prodigious Scepter* is one of the best ships in our fleet," Inga said matter-of-factly. "Now follow me. I'll take you to your room."

Inga didn't wait for them. She merely started walking and the two young women followed automatically. She led them to a stairwell and began walking down the steps. They went down and down and down. It seemed as though they were going to the bottom of ship. They passed several crew members as they went down the stairway.

Wendy and Susie couldn't help but notice that the men seemed to be leering at them but they couldn't tell for sure. Some of them were pretty good looking so they didn't mind.

"I can see why the tickets were so cheap," Susie whispered as they approached their last flight of steps.

Inga shot her a cold look that let her know that she had overheard her. Susie quickly stopped talking.

They continued to walk until they reached the bottom of the steps. Then Inga led them down a hallway to a room at the very end. The hallway seemed to be clean, but wasn't as well lit as the rest of the ship.

"Well, it looks like we have arrived," Inga said and opened the door.

Wendy and Susie went into the cabin which was a lot less than spectacular. It was a small standard room with a bed and small bathroom. There was also a chair and TV. And that was it. To their surprise, Inga followed them in.

"Now, girls, take off your clothes," she said firmly.

Wendy and Susie were taken aback.

"What do you mean?" Susie questioned, although normally she never passed up an opportunity to get undressed.

"It means that you should get undressed. Now. Hurry, we don't have much time. The Captain will be here soon." She snapped her fingers rapidly for emphasis.

The girls were still perplexed.

"But why does the captain want to see us without our clothes?" Wendy asked incredulously.

Inga laughed mirthlessly. "Because you have such wonderful bodies. Now take off your clothes. I need to inspect you."

With that, she pulled out a small whip from her pocket. It was like a bullwhip, but much smaller. It was only about six feet long when it was unrolled, but still looked very intimidating. She gently flicked it just so the girls would see it.

"You're not going to beat us, are you?" Susie said, her eyes getting bigger.

This scene was just not registering it was so surreal. This was just like something in one of movies that one of her kinkier ex-boyfriends had made her watch. She began to get a little turned on just thinking about it. Surely, this couldn't be happening in real life. This was the kind of thing that only happened in tawdry, cheap sex novels with bad punctuation and horrible grammar. While just a little scared, she was also more than a little intrigued.

"That depends on you," Inga said.

Wendy started to say something about how she was going to call the police, but just then the boat started moving.

Then Susie nudged her.

"Let's go along with it. The boat's moving so I think we're stuck. Maybe this is just part of checking in or something," she said, getting more and more turned on by the situation that was presenting itself. She wanted to stick around and see what was going to happen.

Wendy looked at her as if she had lost her mind, but realized that outside of fighting Inga, who would have surely beaten her to a pulp, she really didn't have much choice but to go along.

The two girls began taking their clothes off and could tell that Inga was beginning to get hot and bothered by the way her large breasts began gently heaving up and down and they way she ground the whip into her side. She flicked her hair and walked around them, almost salivating at their bodies.

"Mmmm...yes, girls. Take off everything. Let me see your bodies. Mmmm..."

When the girls were nude, she walked over behind Susie and began to nuzzle her neck.

"You are such a pretty girl," she said in her accented voice. "Such a dirty little thing. You're going to love your cruise experience."

Wendy watched as Susie was immediately wet and turned around to face Inga. Her hands were drawn to the

94

taller woman's breasts and she was soon embraced in a full-on lip lock. It was so intense that Wendy couldn't help but find herself aching to join in. She had seen this girl/girl kissing at parties and clubs, but had just thought that it was something silly the girls did to turn on the guys. This, however, was going beyond any such flirtation. This was full-on sex and she was now aching to be touched.

She went over to them, but Inga pushed her away.

"No. You stay over there and watch," she snapped.

Wendy stopped suddenly.

Inga took the whip and popped it at her leg, making a small welt. "Get back over there and watch or you'll get this," she reiterated sternly.

Wendy was stunned, but was still so turned on that she would've done anything that Inga asked.

Susie went back to kissing Inga and was grinding her pussy on Inga's leg. Inga kissed her neck and breasts passionately and interrupted Susie's grinding to insert a couple of fingers into her vagina. She pulled them out and put them into her mouth.

"Your pussy tastes like a dessert," Inga said. "You taste better than the Hazelnut Napoleons they serve at the late dinner seating." She put her fingers back in Susie for another taste.

Wendy continued to watch, but every time she tried to put her hands between her legs or on her breasts, Inga cracked the whip at her. She made it very clear that there as to be no masturbating or joining in. Wendy was just supposed to watch while she and Susie went at it. Wendy had to consign herself to observing and occasionally sneaking and touching herself whenever Inga was too wrapped up to notice her. Wendy was so horny she would have fucked anything at this point.

Inga stripped off her clothes except for her boots and went to action quickly. She stood over Susie and pushed the girl's head into her smooth pussy. Susie eagerly began to lick her. She lay back on the bed so Susie could get to it easier. Inga no longer had to hold Susie's head because the girl couldn't eat fast enough. Inga groaned as she had a small orgasm. Susie climbed up on top of her and began to suck her nipples. Inga was in complete ecstasy as was Susie. Inga turned Susie around so that she could get a taste and quickly got Susie off. Susie couldn't help but shriek from the pleasure. But Inga wasn't done. She grinned wickedly and produced a large strap-on dildo from under the bed and quickly put it on. It was made of black soft rubber and was around nine inches long. She pushed it down between her legs and rubbed it against her pussy before she inserted it into Susie's pussy.

Wendy was surprised when Inga had pulled the strap-on out. Were all rooms furnished like this? She consigned herself to thinking that Inga had probably put it here for just such purposes, but really didn't really care. She was just aching to change places with Susie.

"There you are, dirty girl," Inga said as she shoved it into Susie's waiting pussy.

Susie gasped and began to grind against it. Inga fucked her hard and it wasn't long before Susie was gripping the bedspread and howling from the orgasm. Inga climaxed, too, from grinding against the other end of the dildo. As she took a breath, she turned to Wendy who was by now almost climbing the walls.

"Now you go over to your friend. I made you wait because I knew that you had not experienced pleasure with a woman and I wanted you to want it. I wanted you to need it. I wanted you to ache for her pussy."

She was right about that. Wendy wanted sex so badly that she was ready for anything that would allow her the release of orgasm. She went over to Susie and immediately began to kiss her neck and breasts.

"Now eat her out, you good girl. Eat the bad girl's pussy," Inga said and cracked the whip on Wendy's bare ass.

Wendy yelped but the pain seemed to intensify her desire. She had never eaten a woman out before, but she was so turned on that she knew that would be a problem. She began to lick Susie's pussy which by now was extremely slick with wetness. Susie moaned as Wendy began to eagerly eat it. Wendy loved the taste of her and could now see why so many women were into it. Her skin was so soft. Just the act of cunnilingus made her horny. She reached down her legs and began to rub her drenched pussy, but before she could orgasm, she felt her hand being pushed away. Suddenly she began to feel Inga lustily eating her pussy. Now, she orgasmed.

"I knew you would like the girls, baby. We all like girls. Some of us just don't know it until we try it." Inga laughed. She then slapped Wendy on the ass hard. "Now, goody two-shoes, I'm going to *really* break you in."

Before Wendy could say anything she felt the dildo being shoved up into her. She turned around to look at Inga, who looked like she was on the verge of another orgasm. Inga had one hand on Wendy's ass and the other rubbing her large breasts as she thrusted.

"Keep eating! Eat like you're at the buffet! Eat like you're a pig!" Inga roared as she fucked Wendy. She slapped her on the ass again hard.

Wendy quickly turned back around and kept eating Susie's pussy. She also rubbed Susie's tits as she ate and was fucked. Susie began to buck again against her face as she had yet another orgasm. This was simply more than Wendy could stand and she had the most intense climax she had ever had.

"AAAAAAHHHHHH!!!" Inga screamed as she ground against the dildo. She was going into spasms with orgasm.

Soon all three women were finished.

Wendy and Susie sat on the bed as Inga began to put her clothes back on. Wendy and Susie started to put their clothes back on too, but Inga stopped them.

"No, you stay nude."

"But we can't just sit around her without any clothes on."

"Of course you can. And you will."

"What about our suitcases? We haven't gotten them yet," Wendy said "These are the only clothes we have."

Inga walked over to the heap where the girls had taken their clothes off. She looked through them and took their underwear.

"No, these are all the clothes you have," she said pointing at their short dresses and flip-flops," she said.

"But what about the rest of our things?" Susie reiterated.

Inga narrowed her eyes at them. "Don't you worry about that."

Before the girls could say anything, Inga turned on her heel and walked out of the door, but before she left, she turned. "The Captain will be by to see you."

She then walked out of the door. Wendy and Susie could hear her lock the door behind her. They turned to each other, still just a little shaky from all the sex they had just had.

"Now, exactly what kind of cruise is this supposed to be?" Susie asked.

Several hours later, the two girls could tell that they were fully at sea by the way the ship was rocking. They were so excited and nervous about what had happened to them and with what was going on that they had been unable to relax. They had also had sex with each other a couple of more times in the interim simply from nervousness and from not having anything else to do. Besides they were both so turned on from before that there didn't seem to be any reason not to. After all, the door had been opened between them so why not walk through it?

Wendy now realized that she thoroughly enjoyed sex with women. At least with Susie, anyway. But she couldn't wait to experience others. If only what was happening to them made sense. It just didn't seem real. And now the Captain wanted to see them. Nude. They were completely baffled.

A little while later, they could hear their door opening. A tall blonde man in his early forties, wearing a white uniform walked in. This was obviously the Captain. He was joined by Inga and an upbeat, short, pudgy, younger red-faced guy drinking a diet coke and wearing a red knit golf shirt and khakis. The shirt was wet with perspiration and, of course, featured the logo of the cruise ship. It was only a few shades darker than his sweaty face.

"I'm Captain Arschloch and welcome to *King Oscar's Protruding Scepter*. I hope that you that you'll enjoy your stay with us, yes?" the Captain said in heavily accented English.

He was typical Eurotrash with a permanent tan and big smile which was only enhanced by his larger than normal whitened teeth. He was the kind of guy who would be at home spending a lot of time in the hot tub. He looked like he was almost trying to be a parody of the typical Hollywood-style American. The fact that he turned almost every statement into a question was a dead giveaway that he was not from Tinseltown.

Wendy and Susie were taken aback. They had been nude when they had entered and were trying to use the dresses to cover up.

"I thought the name of the ship was King Oscar's *Prodigious* Scepter?" Susie asked, pulling the dress over her hips, nervously.

"King Oscar's Scepter is both *prodigious* and *protruding*," Captain Arschloch said matter of factly. "It is just like my penis, yes?" he added as an afterthought and flashed his enormous, toothy smile. "It makes girls like you very happy. And me too, of course, yes?" he said and started tittering like a Teutonic hyena. To him this was as delightful as if someone had told him that he had just won a vacation to Stuttgart.

Susie and Wendy were taken aback by such an unusual statement. And by such unusual behavior.

"This is very true," the red-haired man said excitedly. He was almost like a cheerleader in his enthusiasm. He took a big gulp of the diet soda and smiled at them.

Susie and Wendy just stared at him. Just what was going on here? They laughed nervously.

"This is Skippy," said the Captain, gesturing to the red-haired man and keeping the smile frozen on his face. "He   is the Cruise Director of our ship," he continued. "He will be your supervisor during your stay with us."

At this the Captain smiled even wider and nodded his head vigorously as if he was affirming this statement to a television audience. "And of course, you've already met Inga, yes?"

Inga smiled coldly at them. "And I will be your boss as well," she said.

"Boss? But we don't need a boss," Susie protested. "We're on vacation. What's going on here?"

"Yeah, if you don't let us go, we're going to go to the police," Wendy added. "We paid to be here. This was supposed to be a vacation!"

Inga shot them a cold look and they were silent.

"Oh, it will be quite a supercool vacation and adventure for you girls, the Captain said still smiling. "You were chosen for this position because of the questionnaire you answered. You're really hot stuff, yes? You will be expected to..."

"Wait a second. Position? What are you talking about?" Wendy protested again.

"Oh, you're going to be the ship's sex slaves," Inga said cheerily.

What? Wendy and Susie were stunned. Sex slaves? Their minds reeled. This couldn't be happening. Surely this was a joke.

"But...?" Susie started.

"It's simple," Inga said matter of factly. "The regular girls didn't show up so we had to improvise. You answered the questionnaire in such a way to suggest that you both would be willing candidates to become the ship's whores. Especially the dirty one there with the brown hair." She pointed at Susie. "You passed your test with me so now you will be fucking anyone who wants you. You'll be on call for sex for the duration of the cruise. Whenever a man or woman wants you, you will be expected to provide them your body. No questions asked."

"Sorry about that," Skippy said apologetically. "I wish we could have told you before you came on board, but it's against company policy."

"But this is crazy! You can't turn us into whores!" Wendy protested. "This is illegal! You can't kidnap us like this!"

"Nonsense. Of course we can. Most girls are quite willing once they realize that they do not have a choice,"

101

Inga said. "Especially girls like this one," she said nodding and smiling at Susie who squirmed a little uncomfortably. "And most find they really love it once they realize being a slut is not such a bad thing. Even good girls like you. Maybe not so good any more, though, yes?"

Wendy blushed as she remembered back at what had happened earlier in the day.

Skippy took a sip of his diet soda and wiped his brow with his sleeve. "The great thing is that I'm not hard to work for. Everybody loves me and considers me to be their best friend. You girls will be no exception, I'm sure of it."

After Wendy realized what he was saying, she shook her head. She refused to believe it. This couldn't be real.

"I don't believe you," Susie said. "So if we don't go along, are you going to kill us?"

"Oh, no! Don't be ridiculous. If we kill you, who will service the passengers?" Skippy said, aghast such a question. "We're a team here, after all."

"But you're kidnapping us and that's illegal. You're holding us against our will. You can't do this to us. We want to call the police," Wendy said.

"You can leave whenever you want," Inga said, smiling icily.

"But we're out to sea!" Wendy said. "We can't go anywhere."

"Indeed. I hope you know how to swim. You know I'm surprised that you two girls are so against this, from the way you were with me. It seemed that you loved sex," Inga said. "Your pussies were wet even before I touched them."

"That was different. That was fun," Susie said.

But then she noticed something out of the corner of her eye. Her eyes couldn't help but wander to the noticeable bulge in Skippy's pants. And her libido soon followed. The bulge, surprisingly for a guy like Skippy, was huge and still

102

growing. Even though she was nervous about what was happening, the slut in her couldn't stay buried for long. She could feel her pussy start to tingle.

"Well, this can be fun, too, yes?" the Captain said, beginning to show his excitement. "We can have party right now, yes? Everything will be wunderbar, yes? Let the good times roll, yes?"

Skippy then started rubbing his bulge. "Yes, it will be fantastic," he said taking another sip of the soda. "As long as you can remember that there is no *I* in *team*, this can be a good experience for everybody."

From the ever growing, imprint of his penis that was showing through his khakis, it was obvious that he was very well hung. Even Wendy felt herself getting heated up. A dick that big didn't come along very often.

"So are we going to at least be paid for all this?" Susie said absentmindedly, thinking about what was going on between Skippy's legs.

"You can't put a price tag on an opportunity like this. I think, over time, you'll consider the experience payment enough," Skippy said.

Wendy again shook her head softly. "You're not really doing this to us, right? You don't really expect us to be prostitutes?" she asked, but not nearly as desperately as before.

Her eyes were now focused on the Captain's now protruding hard-on. He had been right, it was protruding and prominent. He was hung, in other words. And it was probably the biggest cock she had ever seen. She could see why he was the Captain. Or at least why people would call him that. Horse-toothed and horse-dicked, a very appropriate combination. She couldn't help but want it inside of her. Her lust was quickly overshadowing her fear and confusion.

No one answered.

Susie turned to Wendy and whispered, "Let's go along with it. They can't really be serious. This kind of stuff doesn't really happen to people in real life. It's got to be some sort of scam they've got to get girls to fuck them."

Wendy was again shocked at Susie's acquiescence but felt herself a little relieved that she was not going to have to turn down this opportunity. While the idea of being turned out was very terrifying, it was also very liberating in a lot of ways. To be compelled to be a slut through no choice of her own was exciting. It allowed her to unleash her sexual beast from the restraints her mother had placed on her. Regardless, she was still hung up on to the idea that this might really be some sort of ruse. She just wasn't raised this way.

"But we can't do this. I'm not that kind of person," she said unconvincingly, her mouth watering at the Captain's cock.

"What choice do we have?" Susie said, starting to squirm at the prospect of fucking Skippy, a guy whom she normally wouldn't even give a second glance. His dick, however, was more than enough to divert her attention from his red, sweaty face and pudgy body.

She took another look at his bulge and before she let Wendy answer, she was already over at Skippy and down on her knees fishing his large dick out of his pants. She had to get started before Wendy did something stupid and made them back out.

As Wendy watched Susie hungrily begin to suck the big cock, she gulped. She couldn't help but bite her lip. It was on.

Inga watched with amusement, her hand going to pussy. She began to rub herself over her pants.

Wendy stood transfixed as Susie worked the enormous dick in front of her. She also noticed that the Captain now had his supersize dick out of his pants. His smile grew even brighter as he stroked himself while looking on at the festivities. Being a sex slave was the most distant thing from her mind at the moment; she only cared about one thing—to get fucked. Her hand went under her dress to her pussy as she watched as Susie worked Skippy's cock.

Susie looked up as she sucked Skippy's big cock. It was obvious that she loved it. It was everything she wanted in a man's member. It was wide. It was long and it was hard. The sheer magnificence of it overshadowed any of his other shortcomings. He also tasted good and she orgasmed a little just from fingering herself as she sucked him. She must have been doing a good job because the precum came fast. She started to slow down, but he held it and let her suck until he knew that she absolutely had to be fucked.

Inga came over and began to kiss Wendy on the neck. Wendy could feel her defenses falling. But she wasn't like this, she tried to tell herself. What about her upbringing? She wasn't this kind of girl. Still the idea of complete sexual abandon loomed large in her mind. Could she be so much of a slut that she could be terrified one minute and completely horny the next? She didn't know, but she knew that as Inga began to caress her body, she was ready for sex. And the Captain's big cock.

With dick in hand, the Captain came over and began to kiss Wendy as well, his big cock pressing against her. She couldn't help but rub it as they began to grind against each other.

"It's just like a big summer sausage," Wendy said amazed at the Captain's genital enormity.

"I can steer the ship with it, yes?" he said, still smiling.

Soon, Wendy was bent over and eating Inga while he fucked her. She was surprised at how easily he entered her, but she was so turned on and wet, the gigantic cock just slid right in.

Meanwhile, Susie had progressed to a full-on boning with Skippy. He was fucking her so hard and so deep that she yelped with pleasure with each stroke. She even had a hard time catching her breath from the pounding she was getting.

The Captain was now fucking Inga while she ate Wendy's pussy. He switched his large dick between the two, providing each with enough stimulation as they sucked each other pussies and tits. Wendy had never been so full of cock in her life and he stretched out every square inch of her pussy. The stimulation was overwhelming because he couldn't help but hit her g-spot with every stroke.

Soon, the action escalated the point of climax and the Captain blew his load all over Wendy and Inga, coating both their faces and their tits. Wendy eagerly cleaned off the Captain's penis as well as Inga's breasts, making sure to swallow. This is something she had never done in her private life, but now it just felt so right. So dirty.

At the same time, Skippy was yelling as he came inside Susie. His face was so red by this time that his head looked like it was about to pop off his neck. He was still holding the can of diet coke. She screamed in orgasm as he filled her up with semen.

When they were all done, and everyone but Wendy and Susie were dressed, Skippy said cheerily as he wiped the profuse amount of sweat off his forehead, "You will be expected on deck in five minutes. Be ready for work!"

Wendy and Susie gasped. They weren't kidding. It wasn't a scam after all. They really were expected to be the ship's sex slaves.

"The customer is key to our success after all," Skippy added.

"Just do what you've been doing so far, yes?" the Captain said, still smiling. "You will have much fun, yes? Like party naked all the damn time, yes?"

"But it didn't say anything on the website about this kind of thing when I booked the cruise," Wendy whined, her horniness wearing off.

"You can't believe what you read on the internet," Inga said. "It lies."

And that's the way it was from then on out.

After their session with the Captain, Inga and Skippy, Wendy and Susie agreed to begin their *assignments* as the ship's sluts. The screwing they had gotten from the three representatives of the cruise line had made the proposition much less reprehensible and much more intriguing.

Once they were established in their new positions, they would walk the ship, drinking, smoking and basically just loafing around, making their appearance known. They essentially worked the ship like it was a floating whorehouse. The term *sex slave* was more of a job title than anything because technically they weren't really slaves. They were more like loose women providing sex on demand. In other words, they were expected to do nothing except fuck and when they weren't fucking or engaging in any other form of sex, they were drinking or gambling or just sunbathing. They would also participate in activities, eat at the buffet, which was called incidentally called *The Captain's Table*, and go to shows, just like the other passengers. It was just like being on a cruise, except for the fact that whenever anyone wanted to use them for sex, they would be expected to comply. Men and women would leer at them and cop feels whenever they felt like it.

At first they had walked around the ship in their dresses and flip flops, but soon, after being randomly fucked in various situations, they let any normal notions of behavior drop. Eventually, after they realized that they were spending too much time backtracking themselves to figure out where they had taken off their clothes, they decided that there was no point of wearing anything other than flip-flops.

Even though they had the run of the ship, Inga still come by occasionally to check on them. They didn't really mind because sometimes Inga would use the dildo on them when she came. That was always fun and they never got tired of fucking the blonde Amazon even though she was never short on condescension.

Wendy had thought she wouldn't be able to handle having sex with all sorts of strange men, but was surprised at how quickly she got over the initial shock. In fact she had found that she was now in a state of excitement almost all the time. She was so turned on that her pussy would be wet almost constantly and she would play with herself often, even in full view of whoever was around. She craved sex and there was no amount of dick that could satisfy her now. This, in turn, led to even more sex for her. And it was all out of her hands. She had been turned into a slut and she hadn't even had to do anything except fuck. The sexual liberation was intoxicating and it felt good to let herself be used. All the women there wanted to eat her pussy and all the men wanted to fuck her.

It was the same way with Susie. It was true that at first they had been a little timid, especially Wendy, but they soon found that they were actually have a good time fucking all these strangers.

After getting started, Wendy and Susie went around together, but eventually were confident enough to work alone. This element really heated things up for them and the unusual settings always made things interesting and exciting. They would have sex in the various bars and casinos and on the Lido deck among other places. Wendy once even had to service a man while he made himself something at the burger bar.

Each day brought new sexual adventures, some of which were pretty weird. One day, Wendy had to have sex with a man who requested that she wear a fake moustache. She didn't really understand what was up with this request, but it really turned him on. And since he was quite endowed and very aroused, she got a really good fucking, which was becoming a priority for her. After she got going, she did not have a problem with any kind of sex no matter how bizarre. She couldn't believe how much she had changed.

All in all, it was a pretty good lifestyle for her. It allowed her to do whatever she wanted as long as she fucked whoever wanted her to. And she could be drunk on the job if she wanted. How many people could claim that perk?

But after several days, the girls began to notice that the buffet was beginning to serve the same meals as it had earlier in the cruise. They soon figured out what was happening. The cruise was coming to an end and the ship was going to be going back into port soon. One afternoon, they were sitting at the Lido deck pool sunbathing in the nude when Skippy came by and told them that they were going to be expected at the Captain's banquet that night. All the passengers would be there and the Captain was going to recognize the crew.

"Make sure you dress to impress," he added.

"But we don't have anything other than those dresses you left us," Susie said. "And they aren't very dressy."

"I think they'll do for what's going to happen tonight," he said, sweating even more than usual.

All day, they sat in nervous anticipation. They noticed that they did not have nearly as much sex as they usually did that day but they figured it was because everyone was packing.

They reported to the banquet that night just as ordered. The Captain and officers were seated on the stage behind a table. Wendy and Susie sat with them, their snatches in full view of the audience. Drinks and finger food was soon served and then the band played a medley of show tunes ending up with a rousing version of *Food, Glorious Food*. This signaled the Captain to stand up and greet the passengers. After he had gone through all the toasts and recognitions, the spotlight turned to the women.

"And what would this cruise be without Wendy and Susie, yes?" he said, his enormous teeth gleaming.

Everyone clapped and whistled crazily.

"And Skippy, yes? Who has done such a good job mentoring these nice girls, yes?" he added. At that Skippy stood up and smiled, his face turning even more red.

The Captain went on, "Since tonight is the last night of cruise, we have to honor the tradition that we have had since we started this sex cruise, yes?"

Everyone clapped even more heartily.

With that a big brass bed with red covers was rolled out onto the stage behind where the crew and officers were seated.

The Captain nodded to Wendy and Susie and motioned them over to the bed. Wendy and Susie looked at each other, not quite realizing what was happening.

"Yes ladies, go over to the bed. You can remove your clothing if you wish, yes?"

"It won't be on long anyway!" a woman yelled from the audience.

Wendy and Susie reluctantly got up.

"Yes, ladies, go to the bed, yes?" the Captain said again. "Because tonight's banquet is not one with food. It's a banquet of sex and you are the main course, yes?"

Now Wendy and Susie understood. It was going to be gangbang and every person on board was going to fuck them. At first Wendy started to panic but she looked over at Susie who grinned wickedly and then got over any nervousness.

"Bring it on!" Susie yelled as she pulled off her dress. "I can take all you fuckers on!"

Wendy stripped off and joined her on the bed.

Everyone laughed and roared with approval. The sound of the unzipping of hundreds of pants and dresses through the auditorium was deafening.

"All-you-can-eat-pussy right up here!" Wendy yelled and rubbed her clitoris, becoming more and more turned on.

Everyone laughed again.

"Everyone take a turn," the Captain said as he began removing his clothing. His enormous dick was hard already. "Remember no cutting in line. Everyone will have his chance, yes?"

With that they started. At first Wendy really paid attention to each person who fucked her, but after awhile, they were all just dicks. It was a never ending supply of cock. It was like a fucking that never stopped. She came several times with excitement after the first twenty or so, but then began to settle in and just take advantage of the sheer volume. The Captain had been first with his huge cock and had shot his wad all over her tits. He had been so big that he really opened her up for everyone to follow. He had fucked her good and gotten her really turned on. The orgasm she had with him was just the beginning or many. Occasionally there would be a break in the action as a woman would climb up on her and let her eat her pussy or would eat her out or suck her tits, but for the most part, it was man after man.

Susie was having the same experience and high-fived her while she lay on the bed and was fucked by a body builder who pounded her while uttering primal grunts. He soon came all over her face and flexed his muscles for the benefit of those awaiting their turn. Skippy and Inga each had their way with them. Inga, of course used her strap-on. It was as though every single person was as horny as hell and fucked them each vigorously. The quality of sex was that good. Each fuck was one that most people would rate as good at worst. Due to this high value sex, each woman had orgasmed so much that they were exhausted and fell asleep on the bed.

A little while later Wendy woke up. It took a minute for her to remember where she was, but soon it all came back to her. She smiled as she looked over at the still sleeping Susie. When she had first gone on the cruise, she had never dreamed she would do some of the things she had done. She had been a good girl, at least somewhat of one, so this had been something that had never even occurred to her even in her wildest imagination. Even after she had agreed to be a sex slave, she had never even dreamed that she would be gangbanged by so many strangers. Such a thing was incomprehensible. Susie had experienced a lot sexually and even this was more than she had thought possible to happen much less for her to do. Wendy remembered what her mother had said about people talking about girls who did the things she had done. She certainly hoped so because she had done stuff that they could never have imagined.

But then Susie woke up. "Man, can you believe we did all that last night?" she said sleepily as she stretched.

"I know. I'm still can't believe it."

Both girls sat in silence for a minute.

"What do you think they're going to do with us?" Wendy asked.

"I couldn't even begin to guess," Susie answered.

"We did everything they wanted us to do," Wendy said. "And I think we were really good at it."

"We were. Skippy even said we had a great attitude," Susie added. "Maybe they'll promote us or something."

"I don't know. But they kidnapped us. Don't you think they're afraid we'll tell somebody?" Wendy said.

"Who would believe us?" Susie answered.

Wendy didn't answer. It was true. What had happened to them was so surreal that it was hard to even articulate it. It was truly like some sort of twisted sex fantasy. And the crazy part about it was that they had gone along with it. And they had enjoyed it.

"This wouldn't have even happened if Inga hadn't been so damned hot," Susie said.

"Or if you weren't such a slut," Wendy added.

Susie looked over and raised an eyebrow.

Wendy looked back and smiled. "Okay. If *we* weren't such sluts."

Both girl started laughing and then went to the burger bar.

Also Available
Amazon.com or Barnes & Noble.com
By Mildred Colvin

Learning to Lean - paperback $8.99
Kindle or Nook - $0.99

She has 3 kids and a daycare. He has 3 kids and is self- employed. They'd be better off as friends, right? Can they learn to lean on God?

Lesson of the Poinsettia - Kindle or Nook $0.99!

She lost her sight. He can't see God's leading when his daughter disobeys to visit the lady with the flowers. Can a little girl and a Poinsettia teach this couple to see with eyes of faith?

A New Life - paperback $8.99
Kindle or Nook - $0.99

She's City! He's Country! She just found out they have something in common. Her son!

Love Returned - paperback $8.99
Kindle or Nook - $0.99

She's in love. But his adopted son could be the baby she gave away nine years ago. If she confronts him, she'll lose his love, and he'll take her son away. If she keeps quiet and marries him, she'll have both husband and son, but be living a lie. Is there a happy ending?

Have **The Ozark Durham Series** sent to your home!

Item	Qty.	Price Ea.	Total
Abandoned Hearts		11.95	
Abandoned ♡'s Study Guide		7.95	
Unexpected Kiss		11.95	
Coveted Bride		11.95	
Cherished Stranger		11.95	
Devoted Mission		11.95	
Merchandise Total			
$3.99 s/h			
MO Residents add 5.85% tax			
Order Total			

Name   (Please Print)

Address

City   State   Zip

Signature (if under 18, a parent or guardian must sign)

Make Check Payable to:
Regina Tittel
Rt. 1 Box 1795
Patton MO 63662

Devoted Mission

www.ingramcontent.com/pod-product-compliance
Lightning Source LLC
Chambersburg PA
CBHW031326170626
46807CB00002B/591